The Ro[y]

THE DROWNING MAN

MIKE WINCH

Dedicated to all my wonderful family and friends who never thought I could write such a novel.

To my good pal Royston Fox who has been waiting for this book for about 12 years.

Particularly to my wife Carole, who managed to stay awake long enough to read it through and correct most or all of the typos and grammatical boobs !

© Michael Archer Winch   May 2023

THE ROYSTON FOX MYSTERIES

THE DROWNING MAN

by Mike Winch

Royston Fox leant casually on the thick wooden railing marking the edge of the safe territory of his balcony cabin on board the Cunard line, Queen Victoria. He had been on cruises several times, but this level of luxury was a new experience for him.... a spot of being spoiled owed to him by the success of his detective business which had suddenly taken off after several years of plodding along looking after insurance claims, divorces and car incidents.

The cruise he'd chosen was actually dual purpose. First as a reward, and second as part of an investigation that had started several weeks before, in a most unusual way.

Royston Fox had started life in the fast lane, rich parents, public school, everything he wanted. Just set to move on to Oxford University, his world fell apart when his father's unwise investments caught up with him in a market crash. His mother left, his father went searching for his fortune in Australia, leaving Royston in the care of his grandparents with little except a very basic subsistence level allowance, and his future in jeopardy.

His love of science was his saving grace having no means of going to Oxford. He was offered and accepted an open place to Southampton University, famed for its physics faculty. He loved the city with its long-standing connections with the sailing fraternity and its yachting clubs which existed all along that part of the coast.

Able to live with two nautical friends renting in a houseboat near Hamble; an old dilapidated minesweeper which in rough weather leaked from the bottom up. The rent was low which suited his shallow pockets, and Royston loved the riverboat life. On the downside he had to make absolutely sure he left nothing lying on the floor overnight. Hanging a pair of wellies from the cabin ceiling, he was always ready to wade through any flood if the worst happened.

Discovering that he could apply for and be awarded hardship funding to add to his meagre means, he knew that he would also have to take on some part-time work to make life a little less basic. Applying to the local police to join the back-office admin team, part-time, he harboured a longer term thought of fully entering the force when he had finished with academia.

This decision changed his life. As his studies progressed, so too did his interest in solving crime. He was allowed to be part of some investigations...

even contribute ideas. Over the three years of his degree, he had realised that although he loved science and would always relish in the curiosity and discipline of problem solving it had taught him, he would not be pursuing an academic career. His future more and more seemed to lie in enjoying the chase and exhilaration of investigating real-life villains and their crimes.

With a first-class honours degree behind him, he was eagerly accepted into the graduate fast-tracking system in the Met Police. He had decided to move to London but finances dictated that he could only live in an outer Borough, in his case Lambeth. Scraping together enough cash for the deposit he decided to buy a late Victorian semi in Streatham, a wonderful building in a terrible state of repair.

Used to working all hours he had managed to complete the essential repairs and updates in six months, and now enjoyed the architectural beauty of all the original features that such a house offered.

Looking back on those difficult early days, Royston had started up the ladder of promotion in the Met, now a Detective sergeant. He had been championed by a more senior officer, Mike McCarthy, who was a man with a huge contact list and major influence in the force. They became good friends almost instantly and worked on several important cases together.

It was at this time that he had the first of several brushes with senior officers. He had insisted on playing a straight bat on several investigations which, because of a desire not to overstep his authority, had incurred the wrath of his seniors who wanted results, even if it meant trampling on suspects rights.

The second time this happened, Royston received a black mark on his record for directly refusing falsely to attribute evidence at a crime scene to the arrested suspect, despite knowing it had been planted by another officer.

At a low ebb, he discussed his problems with Mike, who not very subtly told him that if he didn't toe the line, his long-term future in the force would not be a happy one. His words "the Met stick together" rang in Royston's ears every time he thought about what he needed to do.

Finally, he decided to jump ship and start his own detective agency. Backed by his bank, he leased premises in Holborn and employed an extraordinarily competent personal assistant, Lucy Strike. Together they created a steadily improving company, despite Royston having to accept that for some time, bust marriages, lost partners and bankruptcies would be his trade, maybe with the occasional exciting investigation.

Lucy was a whizz at administration. He couldn't ask

for anything more. Despite their nearness in the office, Lucy always kept the relationship professional. Only once early on, had they overstepped the mark, when after a boozy celebration on the back of winning a sizeable security contract, they had nearly slept together. Royston's long-term girlfriend had moved on and he was again a free agent. Only Lucy's sense of propriety had stopped her in time from falling into an irretrievable situation and potentially destructive relationship.

From then, the line was drawn, and both intuitively understood the limits of their professional friendship. Since that awkward start, Royston and Lucy enjoyed an effective and fun relationship, but life and office never overlapped. This proved to be a workable solution and with the help of Mike McCarthy, the business continued to flourish, being able to survive in the hardest of financial times, and becoming increasingly respected in its field.

Royston left home to travel to the office. It was raining and he could feel the water dribbling down his neck. Just another typical gloomy London day, but with work ahead, he felt all the effort to build his business had been worth it. Very glad to be out from under a massive bureaucracy, Royston now felt fully and in charge of his own life.

CHAPTER ONE

A week earlier, arriving at work in Holborn, he had been startled to see through the open door to his private office, a smartly dressed man sitting there. This had never happened and certainly no appointments would be booked at the start of the day, before Royston had even had time to make his statutory first mug of coffee. Lucy would normally have warned him of such an unusual beginning to the day, but she had not been able to send that vital message.

"Royston!". She looked at him with a discreet sideways nod of the head, which he knew indicated the need for a private word in his ear. They moved into the interview room and closed the door.

"Sorry about this, but he was outside the office when I arrived. He just said he needed to speak to you urgently and marched through into your office and plonked himself down. I couldn't really stand in his way so thought it better to just leave him and wait for you to come in."

"You could have warned me...." Royston frowned, somewhat put out of his stride.

Lucy said sheepishly, "Mobile battery is flat... sorry. "

"OK. What does he want?"

"He said he needed to tell you privately... wouldn't say what it was about."

"That was helpful then." Royston opened the door a tad. "You sure he said nothing?"

Lucy sighed and raised an eyebrow, "Er, yes," she replied sarcastically. "Nadda. He's been waiting for half an hour."

Royston mentally stiffened himself for this interview with the mysterious visitor, and walked pensively through to his office.

"Good afternoon, Sir. I'm Royston Fox.... private investigator."

The man stood up. He was medium height, average build, grey suit but he had a genuinely startling facial expression. He looked as if he was about to explode.... the energy that exuded from his eyes startled Royston into a momentary silence. "Please sit." Royston studied the man in front of him as he lowered himself into his director's chair. "How can I be of assistance?"

The man sat and drew his chair closer to the front of Royston's desk. "I need your help." He seemed to squeeze the words from his lips.

"I think that is obvious!" Royston thought to himself. "What's the problem then," he asked, back in listening mode.

The man moved further forward in his chair and leaned his head towards Royston as if about to convey a deep secret. Instinctively the detective moved his seat further back to maintain some distance between himself and this alarmingly intense person in front of him. "My wife is missing."

Royston stopped himself from raising his eyebrows in mock astonishment. "Oh," he replied with a singular lack of enthusiasm. "What are the details?" He opened the front drawer of his desk and pulled out a note-pad.

"I don't know...." the man screwed his face up as if straining to remember, "I don't know.... she just isn't at home anymore." He shook his head.

Royston scratched his head, thinking to himself that this was just another in a long line of runaway wives, who had needed a life change and had found elicit excitement elsewhere. "Well, it's not unusual for wives to go missing temporarily. Have you two had a row or disagreement even?"

The man reacted angrily. "Do you think I would waste your time if she had just left home after a tiff?" He tensed his shoulders angrily. "Give me some credit!"

"Well actually sir, I don't know who you are, what your name is or where you come from, so if you'd like to explain what you actually want from me, I'll do my best to help. So, let's start with your name...."

"OK..." He paused and took a deep breath, relaxing a little. "My name is Jeff.... Jeffery Turner, and I am a steward on the Cunard line ships. This takes me away regularly, but despite that, Sarah, my wife of ten years, has been a constant support and wonderful companion all that time. Never strayed, never looked at another bloke... to my knowledge...... and always been happy at home and by my side at all times."

Royston made brief notes, thinking to himself that Mr Turner wouldn't be the first husband to be totally blindsided by an errant partner.

"OK. Carry on'.

His visitor drew a deep breath. "I have been away on a med cruise for the last two weeks, on the Queen Victoria.... and when I arrived home three days ago, my wife Sarah.... "Mr Turner took a deep breathe to steady himself, "and everything of hers or connected to her was gone...." He shook his head sadly. "Perhaps I am a stupid blind bastard, but I know that she would not leave like that.... without a word.... it simply is not in her to do that. We love each other."

Royston was beginning to feel a tingling of curiosity. "Absolutely nothing of her left in the house... no jewellery or clothes, you say?"

"I am not lying." Turner again screwed up his face. "There was nothing of her left in our house. It was as if she had never been there. Not even our love letters which she had squirreled away in a secret box in the attic... absolutely nothing. I've spent the last three days frantically trying to find out where she is or at least if she's OK."

"Have you spoken to the neighbours to see if they saw anything?"

"Nobody seems to have seen her, but our house backs on to an alley which is accessible by car and not in view at night.... so maybe she left that way. I just don't know."

"What about family? Have they heard anything of her?" Royston made a note to check the area for surveillance cameras."

"The last anyone heard from her was a week ago when according to everyone I have spoken to, there seemed to be nothing unusual going on. Simply nothing after that." He gave a deep sigh and shook his head.

"Well, what do you want me to do?" Royston was beginning to feel that there actually might be something here other than yet another domestic contretemps. It was extremely unusual for people to disappear without trace or without anyone else seeing or hearing them go... so just maybe this might be interesting enough to spend his time on.

"Find her.... please find her Mr Fox." His shoulders slumped and his head bowed. The fire had gone from his eyes and he now seemed a sad and deeply pained man. "Find her.... please. Her name is Sarah with an 'H', middle name Elizabeth."

Royston took one his business cards out from the pen stand on his desk. "What is her maiden name, Mr Turner?"

"Todd.... Sarah Todd."

Royston noted it down. "Her date of birth?"

Turner screwed up his face. "Err.... October the twentieth nineteen eighty-three."

Royston duly noted the date. "Let me do some initial investigations. My fees are standard and printed on the back of the card." He handed the card over. "If you are OK with those, I can get going."

Mr Turner nodded. "That'll be fine."

"Now then Mr Turner, I can't promise anything obviously, but if you sign our engagement form.... my personal assistant will sort that out for you.... give her all the details you can about your wife and we'll start the ball rolling." He called Lucy into the office, "Can you get the standard form for Mr Turner to fill in and sign, and take all the details from him, please. I'll kick things off using my own contacts."

Royston stood and proffered his hand. "We'll meet in two days or earlier if I have some information. If I have got nowhere, I'll let you know that too. We'll go through every detail at that point. In the meantime, check and re-check at home for anything that might give you a lead as to where she is... and I mean anything."

Mr Turner stood and shook Royston's hand, bowing deferentially as if thanking royalty. "Thank you, Mr Fox....thankyou. I'm not going away again for three weeks so I will be contactable easily enough."

Turner left and Royston sat down heavily on the soggy couch in the outer office. He frowned. "Mmm. Not sure what to make of all that."

Lucy was filing the signed agreement. "He was a bit odd, Royston." She recorded the details on the computer client database with the speed of the excellent touch typist that she was. "That's all done... now it's all yours to solve. She smiled.

"Indeed, Lucy! A very strange man and a very strange problem. See what you can come up with on the internet that might give us something to grab hold of."

CHAPTER TWO

Lucy spent several hours trawling through cyberspace in search of that little something about Turner that might give them a lead or at least a starting point. There seemed to be nothing of any help even after many and varied searches. "Jeffery Turner appears to be who he said he is.... an employee of Cunard shipping." Lucy pushed the keyboard away from her, ... but there is absolutely nothing that says he is or was married to a Sarah and no record of her before or after any marriage, that I can find.... well, not connected to Jeffery anyway. There's a number of Sarah Elizabeth Turner's listed, as well as Todds, but none that seem to fit the bill."

"Well pull up all photos of anyone you can find with those names, and we'll run them past Jeffery and see if any of them are his missing wife."

"Will do boss." Lucy returned to the screen.

Royston picked up his phone and selected the number of Mike McCarthy, his old friend from the Met Police.

"Hi Mike. Royston here."

"Ah, Royston, my old pal. What can I do for you?" He chuckled. "Obviously you didn't ring to see how I was."

"Well, no, actually. I've got a bit of a puzzle on..."

"Nothing new there then, mate."

"No, I suppose not."

Mike was a friend of Royston's brother and had always steered him in the right direction at crucial times greatly contributing to Royston's' current success. Mike, now a Detective Chief Superintendent, with his very useful contacts and sources of information, had sparingly but effectively used them to help Royston, until he had developed his own network.

"Well, what is it this time?"

"I've got a lost wife job." Royston could hear Mike sigh.

"You haven't troubled me on a missing person job, have you?"

"Er, yes and no Mike. I wouldn't bring you in on a simple investigation like that as you well know, but essentially this guy came home three days ago after two weeks at sea as a steward on a Cunard ship, only to find everything to do with his wife, including her, gone from the house. Absolutely everything, clothes, jewellery, pictures, letters, even the marriage certificate and all their domestic records with her name on.... all gone. No message, no trace of when and how she had left or where she had gone. I'd just like to know if either of them has come up on your radar at any time." Mike paused.

"Give me the names then, Royston."

"Mr Jeffery Turner and Mrs Sarah Elizabeth Turner.... maiden name Todd, aged 47, one metre sixty-five tall and sixty-three kilograms. She had dark brown hair, streaked with blonde and generally wore conventional clothes... you know, dress and top or jeans and 'T' shirt. Fit looking and with a Mediterranean complexion. Mr Turner is trying to get some photos from the family for me."

"That would really help, Royston. We could use facial recognition and look at cctv from around their home. See what you can get, and scan and send everything you've got over to me at the office. What's the bloke's name again...?"

"Jeffrey Turner...er... Michael is the middle name. See what you can do Mike. I'll send all I've got over to you including our CCTV footage of him in the office." Mike usually came up with something, but maybe not this time, Royston felt. Jeffrey Turner seemed to be something of an enigma.

Royston lent back in his seat, switching from detective to tired worker thinking about a holiday. He called through to his personal assistant. "Lucy. Can you look for some late holiday offers for me... two weeks somewhere hot and with a golden beach."

"Ok. Any particular part of the world?" She opened the browser on her screen.

"No further than the Canaries, Lu, or the Med." He closed his eyes and thought of golden sands and the warm sun on his skin. He hadn't been away for three years as he struggled to push the business forward, but he really needed a break now. At least he had some spare cash as well as the time to get away for a couple of weeks. He had nearly drifted off when Lucy's voice broke into his daydream.

"Royston why don't you go on a cruise... on Cunard... and you can get a feel for the case at the same time as being spoilt rotten on board?"

"Mmm. That certainly has some merits, I must say. What's available at a sensible price?" Royston's interest was pricked.

"It says here that they have a special offer on twelve days to the Canaries... price looks reasonable if you don't want a suite, you know, a balcony cabin looks good so that you can sit outside and watch the world go by.... and there are midships rooms too, so not too bad if the sea gets a bit rough around the Bay of Biscay." She laughed. "Still, you can always take some seasick pills!"

"Oh, thanks for that. I'm an OK sailor anyway."

"You can have a bit of thinking and planning time. You did say that you wanted to plan our next company move, so now might be a good time."

Royston thought that there was some truth in this. He'd been contemplating an office move away from the busy area they were in, to a more select area in London, maybe even with a few trees. "The world has a habit of catching up with me wherever I am,

Lu, but you've got a good point. When does the ship leave?"

"Well, it's very short notice, hence the decent price.... it leaves next Tuesday afternoon, ...or at least boarding in the afternoon.... actually, leaves around six in the evening. That gives you less than a week to get things sorted. If you don't take too much kit, you could catch a train to Southampton and find a cab to drop you off at the terminal."

Royston made a snap decision. "Book it, Lu. I'll pack later and make sure my papers are in order... I think they are..."

Royston sauntered back into his inner sanctum and checked his email. Several minutes later Lucy called through to him.

"All booked, Royston. I'll print off the details and forms and fill in the bits I can... I've got most things. I'll also get you some dollars... that's the currency they use. How much do you want in cash?"

"Probably about a hundred dollars a day to be safe, although I'll use the company card most times, you have to register that and then use your cruise ID card on board.... so, get me three hundred... that should be enough."

Lucy stood up. "OK boss! I'll pop over to the bank after I've done the paperwork." She left the office.

As Royston leant back in his chair, his mobile phone rang. He put it to his ear.... silence. "Hello....hello."

"Is that Royston Fox?"

"Yes, and who's that?"

"That's for you to guess and me to know...." The voice was light and with a northern England accent, not brash Geordie or Scouser, but probably from somewhere like Derby.

Royston hated cold calls, even more the supposedly clever ones. "Oh, fuck off...please." he flicked the end call button.

The phone rang again...same unknown number. Royston was about to whistle down the phone to put the caller off....

"Don't hang up Royston. I hear you want information on Jeffery Turner...."

Royston took a breath. "What? How do you know that?"

"We have ears my friend... but you may not have, if you continue your search. This is not for you.... oh no my friend. Over your head...... I suggest you go back to chasing errant wives and thieves."

"Stop playing games you dick. If you have anything to say......" The phone went dead. "Shit," Royston said out loud, and scratched his chin angrily.

20

CHAPTER THREE

Royston was in a muck sweat. Suddenly he'd been thrown by the rapid change of importance this new job seemed to have taken on. He now had no idea what was going on, who had done what or who was looking for whom... or why. Was it Jeffery Turner or Sarah Turner... was that even their names? There was nothing he could do until the fog cleared at least a tiny bit.

Most importantly though, after being threatened, he realised that he needed to up his security and keep his communications encrypted if possible. Someone had clearly been listening in at least to part of his conversations. To be honest up until now he hadn't really cared if anyone had, but all that had very clearly changed. Luckily, he had invested in a VPN and a secure telephone line some months earlier on the advice of Mike McCarthy, and after he'd read about how easy it was to break into un-encrypted communications, using freely available software.

He sat at his desk and pondered his next move. Starting his VPN on screen he set up a ZOOM link for Mike and sent it via his local encryption programme to his friend. Mike was the only one with the unlock key. Royston waited impatiently for his friend to enter the chat space... fifteen minutes later he obliged.

"Sorry about the wait, Royston. I had the Commander in."

"Thanks for linking, Mike. I'm really in a mess over this missing woman... I've just been threatened to leave it alone... an anonymous call...." he paused. I don't suppose you have come up with anything to help sort this out."

"Well funny should say that.... the commander has just alerted me to some potential terrorist activity in our area concerning an old employee of the Foreign Office. They think it might be someone who disappeared and has now resurfaced. Nothing specific, but it may be a hidden asset coming back for more.... unknown at this point... I was just thinking that these two snippets of information may be linked in some way. Now you say you've been warned... that kind of confirms it in my mind."

Royston interjected, "but Mike why would a known terrorist or even a connection, draw attention to himself by coming to me?"

"I haven't a clue, Royston, but it would seem that we now need to work together... that is, as long as your security clearance is still up to date and you have signed the current official secrets act agreement? I think you needed all that when you were chasing that bastard ambassador who ran off with one of the British woman staffers some months back, with a pocket full of secrets... Jeremy Clarke C.B.E. wasn't it?"

Royston raised his eyebrows in remembrance of that particular case. "Yes Mike, that was a real eye-opener on the diplomatic service... anyway my papers are in order. So, if that's all I need, can you enlighten me on what the hell is going on, please?"

"OK Royston, but we need to do everything by the book from now on, so come down to the office here and we can work together and record everything... and start with a full update on what we both know so far, however little that might be. I'll clear it with the boss and the terror team... they'll want one of theirs' in the group with us I think." Mike went quiet..." Actually, I suggest we let them set the meeting place and time, so we'll know that no-one will be ear-wigging."

"Fine by me, Mike. Just let me know where and when."

Mike disappeared from Royston's screen. Ten minutes later he reappeared. "OK. Royston, we can meet at one of our safe areas... in Africa House in Kingsway, near you. We have kept some space there ever since the VAT people were turfed out to go to some god-forsaken place in Milton Keynes, many years ago now, and the building was turned into office cum flats... go to reception at 3pm and ask for the old VAT office storeroom. They'll show you how to get there... it's a bit tricky. Shall we say 3pm, if that's OK?"

Royston felt a bit reassured and a little apprehensive, all at the same time. He had met the terrorism people before. They were a breed apart. Totally and absolutely focused on the job at hand and would stop at nothing if they had a lead.

He remembered them after the July the seventh bombings in London... they ruled over everyone who might have even an inkling of knowledge like measles, relentless and completely committed. Now he was about to enter their inner lair and he knew he would have to be top of his game or out he would go. In the meantime, he had to review what he knew and have any paperwork up to scratch. "No scribbled notes now," he thought.

Allowing himself a sandwich from the Sainsbury's local, he sat at his desk and ran through what he knew. That actually was not a lot. He just had a guy off the street who had mislaid his wife. He may or may not have been involved in terrorism or other bad deeds, or he may just have been a bloke whose wife had had enough and left him. That was it.

He read the newspaper, watched the news on TV and then the auction programme to pass time. Nothing new came into his head and he felt that he had to just accept his severe lack of information until someone supplied more. It did worry him though, that Turner had appeared so honest and straightforward in his upset and his tale in general. He didn't seem like a bad guy... but then how could you tell. He had many times felt sympathy for a bad guy who had turned out to be a villain.

At two thirty he left for his meeting. Lucy wished him luck. He felt as though this whole saga was moving outside his realm of comfort. The brisk walk around into Kingsway, past Holborn underground and into the glorious Africa House entrance modelled for a by-gone age. It only took him ten minutes...he was early. He walked slowly up to the front desk and asked the instructed question.

"Wait there sir, and I'll call them down." She picked up a walkie-talkie and spoke quietly into it. "Sit over their sir... they won't be a few minutes."

Royston sat and discreetly looked up for the bank of CCTV cameras he knew must be somewhere as out of sight as possible, but aimed at him. It took a minute to pick out six all at different angles to give a total view of him sitting there. He smiled deliberately at each in turn to show the hidden observer that for sure he knew that they were watching and recording him. It felt unsettling to know, but he tried not to show his intimidation.

At three pm sharp a thick set but immaculately dressed man appeared from round the corner to his right. He extended his hand. "Hello Mr Fox. Please follow me."

They trailed round to the back of the building to what looked like an old service lift, with brass lattice doors and wood panelling on the inside. His guide placed a key into its slot and turned it a hundred and eighty degrees, then pressed a button marked six, slightly to the side of the others. The lift jolted slightly and glided down. Royston counted three unmarked floors and then at the fourth the lift stopped again with a slight jolt. The gates were slid open by a burly looking guy, with well-padded jacket.

Royston flashed a peek at the man's ID tag. "Thanks Mark." The big man nodded seriously. "This way Mr Fox."

He walked through several doors into the brightness of a totally contrasting section of the building. Gone the Victorian extravagance and colour, now bright lights, grey walls and a buzz of activity.

"A bit James Bondy, this" mused Royston to himself. Mike McCarthy appeared from a small office on his left.

"Hi Royston. Nice to see you in the flesh. You just seem to have been a phone call friend lately."

Royston smiled and shook his friend's hand. Mike looked nothing like he sounded he should from his phone voice; medium height, medium weight, very smartly dressed and with black rimmed glasses. "Through here, Royston." He opened the small office door. "Take a pew." They both sat at the small wooden table in the centre of the room. "Jonathan will be here in a minute. He's our liaison with the terror group... nice fellow... very sharp."

The door opened and Jonathan appeared. A small man with busy movements, lots a frizzy hair and a bundle of folders and a laptop under his arm. He plonked the bundle unceremonious down on the table. He was accompanied by a tall blond man in a dark suit and a similarly dressed stocky woman with mousy coloured hair. Mike made the introductions. "Jonathan Bedford, this is Royston Fox... ex-met and now an amazing private detective. Works in Holborn, round the corner." They shook hands.

Jonathan introduced the two people accompanying him. "This is Herr Sebastian Hendell," indicating the tall man, "and this is Frau Schmidt. They are from our German desk and obviously have an interest in the case." They all shook hands and sat around the table.

"Down to action." Jonathan flicked open his laptop. "OK if I record this meeting?" He looked around at Mike and Royston. "OK?" They both nodded.

"Right, this is where we are. Jeffrey Turner popped up on our radar a few years back when he left the foreign office where he was a minion clerk and then vanished from sight. He called himself Jeremy Mooney back then. We follow ex-employees for a while after they leave sensitive government employment to be sure that they stay on side. We couldn't trace him early on so eventually he faded from view, until a month ago when there was an incident on a Cunard liner and his fingerprints and DNA were flagged up as part of the ship's crew. It seems there was an unexplained death... a drowning... and a number of passengers were interviewed... no-one ended up being implicated, but details and samples were taken and listed against what was an unsolved case for future reference. I've checked and Turner was only one of a long list of people spoken to and seemingly of no consequence apart from having his name changed by deed poll before he joined Cunard. That seems to have been the only anomaly, but it rang bells in our system since he had vanished off our radar. So, what have you got, Mr Fox?"

Royston ran through his meagre offering, which now seemed a bit thin. "The only thing I can say is that he seemed genuinely upset and mystified."

Jonathan smiled. "Part of his training I suspect."

The comment struck Royston as a bit harsh. "He did seem genuine enough, Jonathan."

"Not everything is what it seems. Well, I suppose you didn't know that Mike here is a reformed murderer, did you?"

Royston was taken aback and looked at Mike. "What...?"

"Only joking.... Mike wouldn't hurt a mouse, would you?"

Mike coughed and looked embarrassed. "Er... no."

Jonathan smiled. "Where were we… oh yes, never believe your eyes Royston, only rock-hard facts. So, what facts do we have here?"

Mike looked up. "None it would seem but we do have an active link in Turner's visit to Royston and the fact that he does seem to have worked for Cunard. We also know that someone else has a keen interest in the man... we don't know why yet, but Royston at least has a direct contact with the man."

Jonathan interjected," we don't actually know that the man who visited Royston is actually Jeffery Turner or his alias... although from the video it does seem to be him." He fell silent for a moment. "I need to tell you that we were keeping an eye on him because he used to handle some very sensitive papers in the German office. They went mad when we lost him, so now I have to tell them he has turned up. They thought he might be involved in the passing on details of the new drone defence craft to persons unknown in the east."

"So, he may actually be an informer or double agent?" Royston couldn't see it personally. "So why has he popped up in the open spinning his lost wife story?"

"That's what you are going to find out. We are going to slip back into the dark and Mike will be doing the same once we have organised communications with GCHQ."

"Yes Royston." Mike screwed his face up." Yes... I'll liaise with you. You won't see Jonathan again... at least for a while and until we make progress..."

Jonathan butted in." And you mustn't say anything to your staff or friends. All of this is now fully covered by Secrets Act, so absolutely no talking to anyone. Invent a cover story so that your personal assistant suspects nothing... are we clear Royston?" Jonathan fixed his eyes on Royston.

"Absolutely." Royston admitted to himself that he was intimidated by this guy. "I'm off on a cruise... on Cunard... for a holiday, next week. I'll be well out of the way."

"Well make sure you don't draw attention to yourself...eh?

Royston felt a bit irritated by such trivial obviousness. He just raised his eyebrows and didn't say a word.
Bedford proffered his hand and simultaneously offered Royston a business card. "Here's my card… Feel free to give me a ring if you find out anything important."

CHAPTER FOUR

Royston had decided to make contact with Jeffery Turner, if only to find out if he knew what had happened since they had first met. The phone rang…. "Jeffery Turner."

"Hello Jeffery, just touching base to see if you have any more leads… information for me. I've just been doing general enquiries and not a lot back so far. You were going to scan and send some photos for me if you've been able to find any…."

"Hello Mr. Fox." He sounded relaxed. "Like I told when we met, I haven't any photos… but I have contacted her former workplace and another of my friends to see if they can come up with something… but so far, nothing."

"Well, it's a bit tricky chasing someone who you don't have any photos of… or indeed anything else." He cleared his throat. "My personal assistant has downloaded a load of photos of women with the right name for you to look at, but there are a lot. I'll share the pics on Dropbox for you, so you can see and check them. If you can do that asap it would at least eliminate those not to chase up. In the meantime, is there anything new for me?"

"No Mr. Fox." But I will look at the pics when they come through…. Thanks, you are being a great help."

Royston didn't agree, but rung off with a pleasantry, wishing to keep the conversation purely superficial. If this guy was who Mike McCarthy said he was, he would be on guard for anything which might indicate the security forces were on to him. Clearly, he was either very good at presenting a cool head or innocent. Royston didn't know which.

He called through to his personal assistant. "Lucy, I'm going home to throw some stuff in a bag, and sort out any company business so when I'm away things keep running smoothly."

"Well, that's nice." She shrugged her shoulders. "Leaving me here to work my fingers to the bone… fine boss you are." She smiled. "I am going to expect a great present on your return."

Royston grabbed his shoulder bag. "I'll be in tomorrow, but I just need to get up to speed with any outstanding work and emails. I can do all that at home."

"OK. See you tomorrow."

Royston flagged down a cab and gave the driver the post code of his house. The cab silently eased away into the Kingsway traffic. Royston still hadn't got used to these silent electric taxis… he came from the era of smoky old diesel London cabs of yesteryear, in which you sometimes needed to wear an oxygen mask just to survive the trip. He drifted off into thought as the cab zig-zagged through the South London mayhem that led to his home in Streatham.

His home town was changing and not necessarily tor the better with a lot of racial disharmonies raising its ugly head as gangs and groups from far distant places, battled for control of the 'streets' as they saw it. Royston never had problems with people unless they were idiots, and there seemed to be a growing number of those.

"Where shall I drop you guv?"

This broke Royston's revery. "UH… just over there, please." He fumbled for his bank card and paid his dues. "Thanks… great cab!"

Letting himself into the house, a large four-bedroom semi-detached Victorian pile, he picked up the mail from the floor beneath the letter box. Looking through, he sorted out the wheat from the chaff, and going through into the kitchen, chucked the paper rubbish into his recycling bin. Two letters were left from an inch thick pile of post. "Bloody daft waste of trees," he mused. Making himself a coffee, he sat at the island in the kitchen, opened the mail and threw the envelopes away in the recycle bin. "Nothing to deal with there."

He sat, pondering on whether going on a cruise was the best thing to do at this time. After weighing up each side he concluded that a few days away would sharpen him up for what looked likely to be a testing and interesting few months ahead. Not only did he have the Turner case on but he was seriously considering taking on new staff and expanding the agency. Now the Police were so overburdened with social work, more and more serious crime was being investigated and resolved outside the service. Sad state of affairs in Royston's view, but society currently demanded that perspective on life. It made his job even more valuable and he had even considered setting up internationally as it seemed that almost every country apart from the dictatorships, seemed to need help with detection and crime prevention.

Royston jogged upstairs and hauled his big travelling suitcase from on top of the wardrobe. It landed on the floor with a heavy clunk. It seemed he hadn't emptied it since last trip away. He swung it onto the spare bed and opened it up, turfing out all the unnecessary odds and ends left behind from last year. It took him an hour to put everything he needed into the case, protected and bagged, to make his trip easier. He hated folding shirts, and despite being shown innumerable times, still couldn't create the origami style packages that everyone else seemed to manage. He tried… that was it.

Plonking himself exhausted on the bed he shoved the case towards the door, and heaved its bulk downstairs beside the front door. "Job done he thought… except for…"

It took another hour to collect washing kit, passport, other papers, laptop and a bottle of brandy together for his hand luggage. "Now I'm done!"

The next two days were a whirlwind of sorting everything out before leaving. Lucy had found over two hundred potential references and pictures to the missing spouse and had scanned and sent all of them to both him and Jeffery Turner. It would certainly take time to make connections, so Royston didn't push. In all truth he hoped Turner wouldn't come back to him before he left for the cruise when he would have time to deal with it properly.

"Lucy." He called her into his office. "Close the door." This specific room was regularly swept for bugging devices and cameras, just as a precaution. He was feeling paranoid after the security services had appeared. "Can you do me a favour, please?"

She lowered her eyes. "Anytime, boss !!"

"Oh, yes? And you a happily single woman." He smiled.

"Well, you know. Anything to keep the boss happy." She sat down coquettishly.

Royston leant back in his chair and spoke quietly. "I'm feeling a bit twitchy about this whole Turner job, and really want to be sure we are a tight ship. Can you be particularly careful while I'm away and note anything that seems the slightest out of the ordinary. You know, odd phone calls, people following you or appearing in the building unexpectedly…"

"I know the procedures, but I'll be extra vigilant if you think something might happen."

"Yes, Lu. Put all backup disks and sensitive files in the safe today. Keep everything looking normal, but make sure there is nothing of any import lying around or available to be pinched. Report anything suspicious to Mike McCarthy and me. Call him out if you need and in an emergency be ready to make yourself scarce."

Lucy shuffled in her chair. "You're making me twitchy now, Royston. Surely, we haven't got anything on that needs that level of preparedness. Even this Turner case?"

"I only want to make sure you're going to be safe. I'm going to contact Mike to let him know, and make sure he'll be there for you if needed." Royston thought for a moment. "I've covered all bases so things should be OK. Can you get that all done now, before I go, please."

Lucy stood. She knew him well enough and know that he wouldn't act like this without strong reason. She realised that he was very serious even if there didn't seem to be too much of an issue to her. "OK." She left the room as Royston gathered his papers, putting them in his bag and clipping it up.

"Everything secure, boss." Lucy had spent the last two hours locking up the company secrets in their new Phoenix Spectrum safe that they'd installed a month earlier after realising that the old Chubb box could be opened with a teaspoon. "It's a bit full, but everything important is in there… I think."

"Can you double check, and then I'll get off. We're boarding in Southampton at 1.30 tomorrow so I need to be up and about early to make sure I get there." Royston always felt a bit empty when going away for a holiday… almost as if he was about to lose part of himself. He loved his office, his company, his business and his wonderful personal assistant, and it somehow felt disloyal to let her carry the can if anything went wrong. He consoled himself with the thought that he would be in contact constantly via the internet when on the sea, and the phone when he was in port.

"Speak to you tomorrow, Lu."

CHAPTER FIVE

The great thing about going on a cruise was the sheer ease of dealing with luggage at boarding, thought Royston. Having parked in the sea terminal area, he wheeled his luggage towards the great ship docked and lying still in the dock. He trundled his bags towards one of the loaders and left it, walking at a leisurely pace into the terminal building. He checked in and waited patiently to be told when to board. As an irregular cruiser all the enthusiasts were called up first. It made one feel a bit inferior he mused. Finally, he was allowed up the long zig-zag walkway into the luxury of this beautiful ship. He'd mentioned his trip to a few friends who'd either said they were jealous or asked him if he thought he was Hercule Poirot.

In fact, Royston had been on this particular ship before and indeed loved the olde-worlde décor, superb service and relative serenity, which atmosphere a ship with very few youngsters on-board, created.

He was directed to his cabin, a balcony room with plenty of space, neutral colours, king-sized bed, desk, sofa, easy chair, fridge and plenty of wardrobe space. On the eighth deck, he had a great view particularly when they left or entered port. The room had plenty of electric points… the absence of which was the bane of any hotel traveller's life in this world of devices needing charging. The cabins were pompously called staterooms... pretentious he thought, to go with the other Agatha Christie 1920's influences. To him, a state-room belonged in Buckingham Palace.

Royston made contact with his steward, a very pleasant Romanian man who looked more like a wrestler than a ship's steward. "My name is Stephan, sir. Anything you need, please let me know." The maybe foolish thought of calling upon this guy in an emergency, flashed through his mind, especially after the conversations he had had with himself about the potential for violence in the Jeffery Turner case and its security implications.

"Thank you, Stephan… I will."

He emptied his clothes out and placed everything in its appropriate place. Having shoved his case under the bed, he opened the door to the balcony and stepped out to a vision of Southampton docks and the various scurrying boats, tiny compared with his ship the side of which seemed to extend out of sight to each side of him. He liked his midships cabin as it promised the least motion during rough seas. To be honest, the swaying of a ship didn't worry him a lot except when it became violent. This seldom happened on modern liners as they had computer regulated stabilisers, so a little sway was not a problem.

Leaning on the handrail he closed his eyes and took a deep breath…not exactly the salty sea air he had thought about, more dockyard diesel and fug. He returned to his cabin and closed the door. Sorting out his various electronics he plugged the charging leads into the wall sockets. After attaching the phone, laptop, earbuds and speakers, he made a cup of coffee and settled on the sofa. He switched the television on and aimlessly flicked through the channels. "Not a lot," he thought to himself.

He looked at the on-board literature including the day's plan and what would be happening tomorrow and from then on, making mental note of items of interest. He anticipated enjoying the on-board shows and music as well as the wide range of food which was on tap twenty-four hours… a recipe for an expanding waist band. Instinctively, he pulled his stomach muscles tight. He then remembered his promise to himself to go to the gym every day, even for a few minutes. He needed to shape up after a summer of not doing much. He also needed to rest up after his exhausting year… this had to help him recharge his batteries.

He reclined on the bed and dozed off. Wakening with a start, he looked out at the harbour and realised that they had cast off and were now moving slowly round in a circle, guided by the skilled pilot ships, ready to leave the safety of Southampton water. A thrill went through him… he always enjoyed the start of a holiday and particularly a cruise. He returned to the balcony and watched as the huge ship manoeuvred perfectly out towards deep water.

The lights now glowing along the harbour, slid past as the ship moved smoothly on its course. The fast-approaching sunset created a spectacular backdrop to start the trip. The air freshened as the smell of sea air strengthened.

After twenty minutes, Royston returned inside his cabin and dressed in a suit for dinner. He hadn't dressed up for several months. It felt a bit stiff and alien but he actually liked that part of the cruise… the formal dining, proper service at the dining table and even a sommelier to advise on the best wine to go with your meal choice. He had spent some time learning about wines, although he accepted that he didn't have the quality of tasting or smell that made him able to detect subtle differences between similar wines or places of origin. To quote the comedic line, 'he knew what he liked and liked what he knew.'

He was signed up to eat at the early sitting so that he could take advantage of the theatre shows after eating. Having made his way down a couple of decks, he sauntered along the brightly lit corridor lined with select shops. He never felt inclined to buy anything on board, finding the prices a bit over the top. Nevertheless, he looked at the beautiful jewellery on display, admitting to himself that despite the huge prices, to own a piece of such beauty would be wonderful. Arriving at the restaurant, he was directed to a table of six. He was the last to arrive and introduced himself to the party around the table. There were three women and two men, all older than him and looking friendly and communicative. They exchanged pleasantries and gradually eased into communication over the excellent dinner. He had chosen a strong red shiraz to have with his main course steak. The meat arrived perfectly cooked and very tender matching the strong wine flavour as he had been advised. The meal was excellent and he departed the restaurant happy that he would have a convivial time with his new group of friends.

As the ship gently swayed as he was making his way through the large tangle of dining tables, he lost balance and had to reach out to steady himself. Inadvertently his hand landed on a soft shoulder, which when he had readjusted himself, he saw belonged to a small but very attractive woman.

"I am so sorry." Royston flushed briefly. "I lost balance."

The woman raised her eyebrows and smiled. "I've heard some excuses…!" She turned towards him. "It does get a bit wobbly, doesn't it."

"I just lost my balance…" Royston realised that he had just stated the obvious. Embarrassed, he continued to the exit but with much more care. He had to admit that he was more focused on the woman than he should have been. He smiled to himself recalling her pleasant visage. "Maybe…maybe."

He decided to have an early night, but not before finding one of the small bars on board and downing a brandy. Sitting on a stool in front of the steward who was flamboyantly cleaning some glasses and polishing them to perfection.

"Yes sir. What can I get you?"

Royston viewed the bottles ranged immaculately on the shelves behind. "I'll have…. an Otard, please."

"Ice, sir?"

"Yes please… just one cube." His golden drink was placed in front of him. He touched his cruise card on the pay-pad, and rested his elbows on the bar with his drink in one hand, savouring its aroma whilst gently swilling the fluid around the glass. It had a particularly smooth and sweet taste and burnt only slightly as it passed down his throat. He relished the moment and took a deep breath, the tensions of the week sliding away.

As he was internally reviewing the days ahead, glass in hand, he felt a gentle nudge on his shoulder. Startled he looked round to see the woman he had overbalanced into, standing there. "I thought I'd better meet you formally in case you fancy falling into me again…" She smiled broadly. Her perfume pleasantly replacing the smell of his brandy, she sat down next to him... "I'm Michelle. Michelle Baxter."

Royston responded by telling her his name and offering her a drink. She chose a gin cocktail.

"So why are you on board?" She made herself comfortable next to him. "… apart of course, from going on a cruise." She smiled again. "Although maybe with your balance, you were probably meant to be on dry land!"

Royston smiled, taking in her expensive clothes, superb makeup and very acceptable aroma. "I've not been on a cruise for a bit. Not got my sea legs yet." He turned slightly towards his new friend. "So, what brings you here." He blanched internally at this cheesy line. "… I mean are you on holiday?" He realised that that wasn't much better. He cleared his throat.

"I'm here because my husband ran off with his secretary, so I screwed every penny out of him in a settlement… probably not the right way to put that. I now have enough cash to live the life I wanted, luckily now minus his influence. Essentially this cruise is my gift to myself to close that chapter of my life… firmly and finally."

There was sadness in her eyes, which Royston interpreted as the hurt she had obviously been through. "Well, let's drink to your new life." He raised his glass and she reciprocated. "Here's to happy days ahead."

They chatted for another hour and until Royston realised that he missed the performance he wanted to see. The later showing was about to begin… "Are you going to the theatre tonight." Michelle said no, but if he wanted company she wouldn't mind.

They made their way a little unsteadily to the bow of the ship where the theatre occupied a surprisingly large space. They were a bit late but found a couple of seats to one side. The show was an excellent version of a number of West End musical numbers, performed in truly expert manner by the obviously highly able performance team. By the end. Both Michelle and Royston had had a very acceptable evening.

As they left, Royston felt quite an attraction to this woman, but shy of appearing too forward, bade goodnight with a gentle handshake and a suggestion that they might see each other again tomorrow. He made his way happily to his cabin showered and lay back on his bed to watch the evening film.

He woke up having fallen asleep shortly after the start of the film and now with a crick in his neck where his head had fallen sideways as he drifted off. He carefully massaged the offended muscles and woke up enough to turn everything off. Morning came soon enough.

He had decided to moderate his food intake as he felt that if he ate what he wanted, his waist line would expand exponentially. He put on shorts, had a shave and wash and made his way to the Lido restaurant where he could choose a healthy breakfast. He almost achieved that, except for a couple of small croissants slotted in as a second thought at the end. He stoked his metabolism with a strong coffee.

Deciding to sort out his Internet connection and to see if he had emails, he returned to his room.

On board communications were not the high point of Cunard's offerings. It was almost as if the connection was via carrier pigeon, very slow and somewhat flaky. He wished he had set something better up for himself, but he truly didn't realise the situation would be as bad as it was. Exasperated when once again the link was dropped, he swore profusely to himself, deciding to speak to the purser later that day. Eventually after several aborted connections he finished his tasks. Lucy had sent him a cryptic email suggesting that something important had cropped up in the Turner case, but she had not said what.

The ship was not reaching their first port until day three, so he couldn't phone. All he could do was to ask her to encrypt the information and send it to him by WhatsApp or protected email. He felt a slight uneasiness at not knowing what had happened. There was nothing he could do though. Switching himself into holiday mode, he made for the ballroom, having decided to revise and update his dance skills. He had always loved dancing and enjoyed the televised dance competitions immensely, sometimes envisaging himself, somewhat vainly, as a participant.

There was a large group of the fit, the able and the hopeless. He assessed his chances of being trodden on, and made for a place on the dance floor which looked to be a relatively safe place for him to try his skills. The eastern European dance teachers spoke loudly and deliberately to the gathered throng with infinite patience. At least half the dancers did not have an ounce of rhythm and the other half had turned into 'tutters', sometimes loudly proclaiming their desire to boot their inferiors off the floor. The whole hour, was however, much fun, and he had gradually relaxed into the rhythm and movement he loved to feel when he danced.

In need of lunch, he again made it to the buffet, this time just selecting things he really liked to eat… plenty of seafood, crispy bread rolls and a small selection of cheeses. Time for a nap, he decided as he made his way, with a yawn, to his freshly cleaned cabin.

CHAPTER SIX

That evening was to be one of the formal Ball nights, the Black and White. That meant that everyone needed to dress in black and white, but poshed up and glamorous. Royston had brought his Tuxedo with both jackets, so he decided that probably, to be a bit different he would use the white jacket, black dress shirt with white bow-tie. Having refreshed himself with a shower and a brief stay on his balcony letting the wind blow the cobwebs away, he was beginning to relax. "Right," he thought to himself. "Let's get this bloody internet working."

Sitting at the desk, he logged on to the network. "Come on…. Come on." Eventually he had a stable connection. He sent an encrypted message to Lucy asking for an update. To his surprise, he received a quick answer back.

"Mike says be careful. There has been some traffic on the communications front. He is unsure whether it is relevant, but said to be on the lookout."

Royston responded that there had been nothing untoward going on so far, but yes, he would be very careful. "Has there been any contact from Jeffery?"

The answer came back. "Nadda."

"Well let me know instantly if he raises his head."

Lucy again responded immediately. "OK, boss. Be careful."

Royston signed off, not unduly worried about the caution to be wary. It was his second nature as a detective to notice the slightest significant nuance as life swirled round him. He decided that a pre-dinner drink would go down well, half hoping that Michelle would be having the same thought. She had made quite an impact on him.

He dressed, made sure everything looked good, and stepped out into his corridor. There were two people walking away from him talking. Immediately his hackles were raised… did he recognise that voice. He told himself not to be so paranoid and suppressed the urge to step back into his room. The voice was Northern English like the threatening phone call he had received back in the office. He took a deep breath and walked purposefully up to the group, as he had to, to get to the lifts. "Excuse me."

The group looked round at him. "Oh. Sorry." The two stepped back to wall and let him pass with a smile.

Royston relaxed and un-hunched his shoulders. "It just shows how tense and on edge I am," he thought, mentally chastising himself for his mistake. He reached the bar and plonked himself on a stool to one end.

The bartender flashed over to him. "Sir?"

Royston had already decided on a Long Bloody Mary… healthy but sparky.

The bartender busied himself splashing the components skilfully into a shaker, test tasting the result, adjusting the contents and then delicately sliding the red liquid into a tall crystal glass which had a small amount of crushed ice in the bottom and a delicate glistening rim of salt and pepper. He handed the result to Royston with a raised eyebrow.

Royston accepted it happily, sipped and smiled. "That's great." The bartender responded brightly. "That's my job."

He sat and contemplated this relaxed life as the ship almost imperceptibly swayed a little to the left and then to the right, to the slow rhythm which reminded him of days spent in his youth, floating on a Lilo in the sea at Littlehampton on a scorching summers day. He drifted into reverie, closing his eyes momentarily.

Michelle's perfume preceded her. "Why hello, sailor." She smiled as he snapped back into real time.

He looked up, smiled and attempted with some difficulty to pull the stool next to him a little closer. "Hi Michelle. Here for a beer?"

"No. Something with a bit more zing…. The bartender had instantly materialised with eyebrows raised and ready for her order. "Tequila sunrise please."

A couple of minutes and many manoeuvres later the drink arrived, from bottom to top the traditional red to orange. She sipped it gently.

Royston realised he was gawping at her in a most juvenile way. "She really is lovely, he thought," slightly flushing. He cleared his throat and sat upright a little more formally. "Is that OK?"

She flashed a smile at him. "Fab. I love these. Make me squiffy if I overindulge though…." She looked at him, "…. better be careful!"

Royston sipped his drink. "I saw you were sitting with a small group for dinner. So am I. Would you like me to see if either of us could move to one of the tables?"

"That'd be an idea." Michelle responded. "The folk I am with are not friends, just a group I was put with. So, I can certainly move."

"Likewise. Let me speak to the restaurant manager. She's great." He paused. "I can speak to her when we go in tonight." Royston was definitely buoyed by this idea. He was beginning to feel more than a little attracted to Michelle." He mentally chastised himself for being way too forward. "Settle down, Royston. Settle down."

After another excellent cocktail, they sauntered along to the restaurant and made their way to their separate tables. Again, the dinner was excellent and the conversation fun. In a way, Royston would be sad to move away from this jolly group of travellers who had made him feel so welcome. It hadn't happened yet, so he put the thoughts aside and enjoyed his meal. He went a bit mad on a very expensive white wine, but didn't count the cost… it was beautiful.

Wishing everyone a good night, he made his way toward the restaurant entrance. He was careful not to wobble into Michelle again, who smiled as he passed. The manager was standing at the desk in the restaurant entrance. She was talking to one of her staff. Royston, waited patiently until she had finished. She was a tall woman, immaculately dressed in staff uniform and hair in perfect balance. She was middle-eastern, with the grace and poise of the women from that part of the world.

She looked at him.

"Would it be possible for me and my friend to sit at a table for two, in dining?" Royston asked.

"What are your tables, sir?"

"126 and 312". Both tables are for six. There's nothing wrong with either, it's just that we thought it would be nice …." He left the ending open.

The manager looked down at her table plans and scratched her forehead in thought. She spoke quietly to one of her staff who replied equally inaudibly. "Well… I think we can help. We have an unexpectedly available table down at the back in the right-hand corner, if you'd like that?"

"I think that would be fine. What table number is it?"

"428. What are your room numbers?"

Royston realised he didn't know Michelle's. "Mine is 8018 and er…." He paused, looking around. "Michelle what's your cabin number."

Royston went to her table. The restaurant manager wants your room number.

"That's convenient… for you." She laughed. "4036."

Slightly embarrassed, Royston returned to the desk. "4036."

The manager wrote the details into her restaurant plan. "I'll speak to the waiters and sommelier to expect you from now on. Could you ask your partner to sign in with me, please."

"Partner?" Royston mused to himself. "I'd be so lucky." He again made his way back to where Michelle sat and explained what the manager had said. She appeared very pleased with the arrangement and said that she would check in at the desk on her way out.

Royston didn't want to hang around at the table. He told her that he was heading to the bar in the Winter Garden, a large elegant room at the front of the ship's upper decks. Next to one of the swimming pools which was lit at this time of the evening. A sparkling sight. There was a good band playing, who covered a wide variety of hits over the last forty years. They managed to keep the volume within reason and their skilful playing made it a very pleasant entertainment either for sitting and listening or dancing to.

He ordered another Bloody Mary and sat and waited impatiently, he had to admit, for Michelle to arrive. He looked through the next day's activity sheet and the flyer with possible landside trips detailed.

"HI there!" Michelle put her hands over his eyes from the back. "Guess who?" She laughed and sat down next to him. "Who's the band? They're good."

Royston cleared the table of his paperwork. "It's the house band… and pretty good they are too. Good choice of songs."

Michelle ordered a cocktail from the waiter who had spirited in from nowhere. "This is fun!"

Royston looked at her. "I know this is a bit corny, but tell me about yourself."

Michelle looked down. "Well… I told you about my split up… before that, I worked as part of an IT team developing AI software in Canary Wharf… you know facial recognition, number plate ID and all that. I have gone back to that and found a great little apartment close by, well not so little... but felt I needed a breather… to settle myself. So here I am on this cruise" She gave a slight shrug of her shoulders, the weight of her recent emotional trauma seemingly weighing her down. She shook her head. "He really was a complete bastard… difficult to get him out of my head."

Royston realised he needed to lighten up. "Well, you've got rid of him, so here's to a happy, free and exciting life from here on in." He raised his glass and chinked it on hers. She relaxed, sat back in her chair and closed her eyes. "Alleluia to that, Royston."

Royston moved the conversation on to what off-board trips he was thinking of doing. He intended to go to the superb Madeira shop in Funchal as well on some of the tours set up for the other Canary Islands. Funchal, though was the first stop on the Island hop, and Royston had moved from being a Madeira denier to a real enthusiast. The deep and subtle taste seemed to grow on you, and now Royston numbered it in his short list of essentially favourite drinks.

Michelle, wasn't fussed, even after a lyrical ear-bashing on the drink's subtle majesty. "It's OK." She deliberately played her enthusiasm down and smiled. "Me, I'm a champagne girl."

They sat chatting for another hour, before retiring to their rooms. Royston tested an arm around her shoulders, feeling an immediate reaction, he withdrew it.

"It's ok Royston." She looked round at him. "I need to get back into being comfortable with men." They arrived at her deck. She gave him a gentle kiss on the cheek. "Night-night. See you in breakfast early. eight O'clock?"

"Yeah, fine. See you then."

As he made his way up to his cabin, Royston admitted to himself that he had really enjoyed the evening and wished he hadn't been so pushy. Michelle was obviously very fragile emotionally and he realised that he must tread very carefully.

He slept well that night starting to enjoy his break. All thoughts of the Turner case had for the moment been shelved.

CHAPTER SEVEN

Bleary eyed, Royston peeled himself out of bed. With one eye, he looked at his watch… seven thirty. He remembered he was to meet Michelle for breakfast. Suddenly alert, he rushed to ready himself. He showered, shaved and generally smartened himself up more than usual, finishing up with an approving glance in the mirror all in the space of fifteen minutes.

He walked quickly through to the self-service restaurant, looking for Michelle as he made way unsteadily along its length. There was quite a swell which rolled the ship unpredictably, not enough to make plates fall off the tables, but enough for him to want to sit down and re-attach himself to Terra Firma. Passing unsteadily across the ship into the other side of the restaurant, he spotted Michelle seated at a window table looking out to sea.

Steadying himself by holding the backs of dining chairs, he reached her table and sat down. "Definitely a bit rough today."

"We're in the Bay of Biscay… always dodgy here. I'm an OK sailor though. Never troubles me."

Royston shrugged. "I'm not sure if I can say the same. I tapped my GP for some anti-sea-sick pills just in case. I think I'll be having one after breakfast."

Michelle looked concerned. "Go out on deck in the fresh air if you feel bad. Focus on the horizon… if you can see it... and breathe steadily. That usually works, I'm told."

"I'll settle for pills." He unwrapped his napkin and spread his knife and fork. He paused. "I think It'll be just toast and tea for me."

"Well, I'm having a full English." She smiled and stood up. "Anything I can get for you?"

Royston puffed his cheeks at the thought of fried food. "No thanks. I'll go for mine when you come back."

As he followed her progress towards the food, he noticed the two men he had seen two days earlier outside his room, who he thought might be hostile. They were deep in conversation with one of the ship's officers, or at least Royston assumed he was an officer. He was dressed in white with insignia on his shoulder and the front of his shirt. Royston hadn't a clue what rank he was, but thought he had seen the man in the purser's office on deck one.

The group looked serious and occasionally looked round furtively as though worried that someone might eavesdrop on the conversation. Royston instinctively looked away as he saw one of the men start to turn towards him. He couldn't pinpoint his worry, but worried he was. He discretely manoeuvred his mobile into a position from which he could take some photos of the group, twice having to abort as one of them looked around in his direction. It was difficult as they were in an alcove shielded by a glass partition, but eventually Royston was satisfied that he had all of their faces clearly on file.

Michelle arrived back at the table. Royston avoided looking at her plate of food and went off in the opposite direction to the group of men, to find his meagre breakfast, returning some minutes later. As he enjoyed his food, he noticed the men were no longer at their table. Royston immediately felt less tense. Michelle deflected his thoughts and by the end of breakfast he was back to normal.

"What's your plan for today, Michelle?"

She pursed her lips. "Not a lot. Thought I'd go on-line and contact the family. I haven't spoken to them since we left. They'll think I've drowned or something." She laughed. "Mind you, if it gets any rougher I probably will." The weather was certainly building up. "I've got a practice with the choir this afternoon. Great fun, and then some pampering with a massage."

"What choir's that?" Royston was a bit surprised. He hadn't figured her as the formal singing kind.

"Yeah. They advertised it in the daily 'what's on' sheet. The first one was great fun, and on the next to last day we sing in concert format for anyone who wants or can bear to listen to us."

Royston hadn't seen it advertised.

Michelle looked animated. "We're doing six songs from musicals… all great fun. I haven't sung for ages, but it all comes back quickly."

Not wanting to be pushy Royston said he'd meet her at dinner in the evening as he needed to do some work on cases he'd been avoiding for a couple of weeks. Humdrum but provided bread and butter money to keep the company up and running. He made his way back to his cabin. As he entered the corridor, he was startled by the ship's officer he'd seen earlier in the dining room, who pushed past him in great haste and disappearing into the lift lobby.

A bit ruffled by this encounter, he entered his room and opened the curtains that were drawn across his balcony window. He was starting to feel really low, despite the sunshine Michelle had brought to him. The rain was lashing across the table and chairs outside. Sitting down at the desk, Royston opened his laptop and turned it on. He waited for it to boot-up, tapping his finger with impatience. The machine chugged slowly into life and eventually displayed the log on box. He obligingly completed the request for a password and again the laptop seemed be in slow motion. Eventually it was set for Royston's intended interrogation.

He opened the browser and started typing in his webmail address. Immediately a warning was displayed by the anti-virus software. "Your computer has been attacked by generic boot sector virus 25117b. Close down immediately and re-boot in safe mode. Run a full antivirus scan."

"Shit… It's this bloody useless internet…" Royston knew it wasn't, but he had nothing else to blame. He closed his system down and did as he had been instructed. Forty-five minutes later, virus removed, he was back at the beginning. He didn't much feel like trawling through the notes he'd prepared on a rather boring matrimonial case, and drifted into surfing the net for Cunard Officers. He looked for the insignia he had seen on the dining room man. Nothing caught his eye. Finally, he gave up and decided to send copies of the photographs he had taken, to Mike McCarthy at home. The system seemed even slower… eventually the information was transmitted back to the UK and Mike confirmed he had received it.

Feeling very frustrated he made for the pub in midships and sat at a table looking out to sea. He ordered a beer and a curry for lunch, comfort food and drink… He sat on his own feeling stressed and irritated, not exactly as he had aimed to be three days into the cruise. He couldn't pinpoint why he was feeling this way, although he had to admit that a number of the unexplained minor incidents could easily have had perfectly innocent explanations.

A second pint and he was feeling a little more sanguine. The ship had nearly stopped rolling and the weather outside had markedly brightened. Beams of sunlight were streaking down onto the sea and with this came a lightening of the skies, so too did Royston's spirits start lifting. He realised that being suddenly away from home, he'd started internalising his own worries... he was in essence depressed, trying to explain it and fighting his own demons. It had happened before after a serious challenge to his identity had forced him to descend into an ever-tightening loop of self-criticism. Then, he had fought desperately hard not to go too far down... he only just succeeded by seeking advice from a fellow police officer, Mike McCarthy. Mike had steadied his spirit and talked him through strategies to cope, which eventually had become a normal pattern for him in times of stress. Now was one of those times.

As the burden lifted, so too did the clarity of his vision. He realised that he needed to nail down the identity of the officer in white and his friends. He logged onto the web on his phone and then his webmail. Mike had replied to his query about the photos. "Faces not on database so have passed it up the line to Jonathan. Will message if anything found. You should know...Turner's been found dead in the Thames. No suspicious circumstances apparently but it's being thoroughly investigated."

Astonished and now more than a little frustrated. The main man in the case now dead. Royston decided to go and watch Michelle's singing rehearsal in the "Yacht Club" on the tenth deck. He arrived in mid-song which to be honest sounded pretty good to him. He sat at the back and let his mind drift off as the choir went through their repertoire. Michelle had noticed him and gave a discreet wave and smile. By the end, Royston was drifting off into a daydream.

He didn't notice Michelle come over to him, until she prodded him. "It wasn't that bad, Royston, was it?"

He started. "Er… no it was great. I was just thinking about a case… sorry." He needed to back this up, he felt. "It really did sound good, Michelle." He knew that didn't sound very convincing.

"Yeah, yeah!" She playfully pushed him into his chair. "You were asleep for the second half and weren't here for the first. Anyway, it did go very well...I think." She sat down next to him. "Do you fancy an afternoon tea before I have to go to the Spa?"

"Great idea. Let's go." Royston stood and stretched. "Shall we go to the ballroom. Tea is very English there even if the sandwiches are miniscule."

She took his arm. "It'll help you to lose some weight."

"Ho ho!" Royston pulled his stomach in, instinctively. "Let's go."

Michelle pressed the lift call button. "You're looking a bit pensive Royston. Anything the matter? You haven't got a hidden wife, have you?"

"No. No. Nothing like that. I've just started seeing things that seem suspicious…"

Michelle nudged him to enter the lift. "Well, you are a detective. That's your job, isn't it?"

Royston felt embarrassed. "Well yes, Michelle. But there may be a connection with a case I've just started…" He paused. "Or maybe I'm just seeing things and people that are not connected. I'm not sure."

Michelle gave a visible shudder. "What, you mean the case is connected with this ship… now? That's spooky."

Royston didn't feel he should go into much detail, so he deflected the question. "It's just that I've seen some blokes acting suspiciously near my room, and a ship's officer talking to them. I took some photos and sent them home to see if I was talking rubbish."

"What, you mean get your pals to do Facial recog on them? Didn't you remember that that particular game is my speciality… I'm the queen of FR. Send me the photos and I'll get my team to do a trawl. Far better than the police databases."

"That would be great as so far my contact has come up with nothing." Royston wasn't sure but it was worth a try, even if it was just to see what she could offer on this score.

"I'll come to your room after my massage, and we'll go online… yes? What's your cabin number?"

Royston hesitated momentarily. "Er… 8018."

"See you after my pampering." Michelle left the lift and blew him a kiss.

Royston continued down to deck one to head for the Purser's office. He was desperate to sort out a better broadband connection.

CHAPTER EIGHT

As usual the staff in the Purser's office were polite and helpful, explaining that the ship's communications were satellite based and had been interrupted by the bad weather. This seemed a bit of a feeble explanation for a multi-billion-dollar company. Surely, he thought, a system that worked well and cheaply, was possible.

Not particularly satisfied, he pressed a little harder to see if things could be improved.

"I'll let you speak to our Communications Officer, sir. Wait here, I think he's in the back office." The receptionist turned and disappeared through the door behind her.

Royston waited patiently until the door re-opened and the woman emerged.

Royston was momentarily startled as he saw who was accompanying her… it was the officer in white. As their eyes met, there was a definite flicker of recognition, instantly shut down.

"Good afternoon, sir. I'm Mark Procter.." He looked down at his ID card as if to reassure himself. "...the ship's communication officer." He smiled. "I hear you are having Internet issues."

Royston had to take control immediately so as not to demonstrate any recognition of the man. "Well yes actually. The connection has been inordinately slow since we left and I wondered, since I am paying a hefty price for the service if anything could be done to improve it." He smiled, realising he was being a bit too aggressive. "I need it, to stay in contact with my business at home."

"Well, we are having trouble due to atmospheric conditions Mr Fox, as my colleague has explained." He turned and glanced at the receptionist. "I'll send a technician up though, to check the nearest router to you. They are in the lift lobby. What is your stateroom number?"

"8018."

The receptionist noted the number on a slip of paper and handed it to the Officer who looked at it and put in his pocket. "I'll see someone gets there as quick as possible Mr. Fox. When might be a good time when you are in, so that the technician can test out the connection?"

"Now?". Royston had reacted internally, realising he hadn't mentioned his name. He flushed, feeling his ears redden. Maybe the officer had checked him out from the back office. "Stop being so bloody paranoid," he chastised himself. There had been no hint of anything unusual or suspicious with the conversation, in fact the opposite. The response had been perfectly normal and friendly.

The officer flicked a clip file of schedules, and looked up. "I'll send someone up now."

"Thanks. That's really appreciated." Royston turned to leave.

The Mark Procter smiled. "It's my pleasure, sir."

Royston made for the lift, a little irritated with himself for displaying his emotional response. Arriving at his room, he made a coffee and set up his laptop. It chugged into life… he tried the internet… still slow. He sat back and took a sip of his coffee, swearing as it scalded his upper lip. "Jeez…." He went into the bathroom and doused his mouth with cold water.

Returning to his desk, he logged onto his email. After what seemed an age, the connection was made and a slow scroll of messages appeared on screen. Trawling through them, deleting the rubbish or uninteresting, his eyes lighted on one from the office, in fact Lucy specifically. The message was light and breezy and full of her daily work and conversations…

There was a knock at the door. He closed the email down and went across to see who it was, although he assumed it would be the internet technician. As he opened the door he was pushed back violently, losing his balance and falling backwards onto the floor. Somewhat dazed he heard the door close, and then tried uselessly to resist a strong grip around his neck, which paralysed him from struggling. A few seconds later, he felt his arm being bared and a sharp prick of a needle in his forearm…

Royston came to, on his bed. He had a terrible headache and there was a small spot of blood on his arm marking the spot where he assumed a hypodermic needle had been inserted. Groggily, he tried to stand and immediately pitched forward into the wall. Steadying himself, he managed to reach the toilet before vomiting violently until he was just retching.

He cleaned up the mess and showered unsteadily, nearly precipitating himself into the mirror opposite the shower as he emerged, in a sad and sorry state. He again steadied himself and only then looked around at his room, or should he say what was left of his room. Nothing had been left untouched or unopened. The remains of possessions were lying crushed in the main, on the floor. His laptop was gone, his phone, wallet and jewellery all no longer in their allotted places, and his clothes torn and trampled on.

Sitting on the end of his bed, Royston pondered on the wreckage. He reached for one of his pillows and felt deep inside, giving a sigh of relief as he pulled out his passport and a wad of currency. It was an old habit of his when visiting dubious hotels, to hide his key items in the bed, as no-one bothered to look there when attempting a robbery. Although he hadn't considered the ship to be in anyway dodgy, he hid the items through habit. At least he had the main elements of his life even if the holiday goods were trashed.

He phoned through to reception and asked for security, explaining briefly what had happened. Within a couple of minutes, a swarm of security and other officials appeared at his door. He was a bit overwhelmed. Not only was he escorted personally to the sick bay and examined from head to toe, but he was then upgraded to a suite of immense size. Not really wanting all the fuss, he explained that everything would be OK after a good night's sleep. The room stewards fluffed around him asking what clothes he needed and whether he'd like room service to provide something for him to eat or drink.

All he really wanted was to be alone and get back to reality. His head was splitting and nausea kept poking its head up from below. "I'll be fine, guys. I just need some water and to get some rest."

The head steward of the group, nodded. "Yes, I understand, sir… but the security chief would like to speak to you now, if possible, while the memories are fresh."

Royston smiled weakly, "What memories? I haven't a clue what happened. I'm not really up to it, but if he thinks it's important though, of course I'll speak to him." He walked over to the large desk and its comfortable chair. He raised his eye brows at the opulence of his new living space. Looking at his bare wrist, it took a few seconds for him to realise that his watch had also been stolen. "Bastards," he muttered to himself. It had been a timepiece given to him on graduation by his grandma, a truly lovely and most wise and influential person in his life. He valued that watch more than any other, as a reminder of her happy smiling face.

There was a knock at the door. One of the stewards responded. An ultra-smartly dressed man of six feet four stood in the doorway, his white uniform gleaming and every part of his attire immaculate. "It's OK lads. You can finish later." He gave a slight sideways nod of the head. The stewards exited sharply. "I'll let you know when I'm finished. He closed the door after them.

"I am Brigadier Blackstone, Mr Fox. Security chief on the ship." He walked across towards Royston. "May I sit down?"

Royston nodded. "Yes, fine."

"You obviously know why I'm here. This is a terrible thing to happen and absolutely unheard of on one of our ships. It is both in your and our best interests to find out what happened." He opened the folder he was carrying and took the silver pen from his inside jacket pocket. "Can you tell me what you can recall… right from the beginning?" He looked at Royston.

Royston's brain was still fudge. He went blank…"Err… well… I can't remember anything except answering the door and being nearly strangled and injected."

"How many were there?"

"I haven't a clue. I was completely taken by surprise. I have presumed two… one to grab me round the neck and the other to give me the jab. I caught a glimpse of one of them who had a black balaclava on, so I couldn't even tell you his eye and hair colour… I can't remember anything useful." Royston really couldn't remember anything significant, not even a smell or a voice.

"What did they say before you answered the door?"

"I didn't ask." Royston felt foolish at this childish mistake. "Sorry, but I didn't expect to get attacked on board this ship."

The Brigadier shifted uncomfortably in his chair. "No, I understand that… and neither do we expect that to happen either, not on this shipping line." Back to business. "Can you fill in this form to list all your stolen items… absolutely everything including clothing. We will replace everything… new…" He paused. "I really am sorry Mr Fox. I have no idea who this was, but I am damned sure I am going to find out. We have an investigative security team on board, who are going to go through your room with a tooth comb to see if they can pick up any clues or forensic evidence. The thieves are still on board, but we need to find them before they can disembark tomorrow morning when we dock at Funchal."

Royston did not want to extend the idea that they were probably not thieves, but part of the group who had threatened him before he came on board. They'd be looking for anything he had on Jeffery

Turner, where he was or how they could get at him. Royston also did not want to let on that he was a detective… that might just create more problems. Better let the ship's team deal with it. He may even learn something himself about the men who had tried to intimidate him, and were after Turner.

The Brigadier left, promising to update Royston on progress and ensuring him that he was secure in his new suite, with an extra watch being put on the deck.

Sitting back, Royston's throbbing head started to ease. He leant back in his seat and closed his eyes. It had been a blur, and he now wanted to return to as close to normal as possible.

Suddenly he remembered Michelle. He started, remembering that he was supposed to be meeting her after her spa treatment, for a cocktail. She'd be worried stiff when she found his room empty and possibly full of security staff. He dialled her room

Michelle answered, Royston thought a bit shakily. "Hi Michelle."

"What happened, Royston? One of the stewards said that you had been attacked and robbed in your room…are you alright?"

He didn't want to scare her. "Yes, I am OK. A bit worse for wear, but nothing I can't handle. They were thieves and they trashed my room and stole a load of stuff."

"Oh, Royston." She sounded tearful. "Can I come and see you?"

"Of course." He gave her the suite number and deck. "Come on up and we'll order room service for dinner… and definitely a decent bottle of wine. Come up at seven. That'll give me a chance to rest for an hour and dress. I have one serviceable shirt and a suit. So nothing smart I'm afraid!"

"Are you sure you're OK, Royston?"

"Yes. I'm fine, just a bit shaken. See you at seven. Don't worry." He put the phone down, hoping that Michelle was not too shaken.

CHAPTER NINE

Royston flopped on his bed, exhausted by the days experience. Falling almost instantly asleep, he dreamt through the recent attack over and over until he woke with a start. There was a knock at the door. Immediately he was alert and ready for anything, adrenaline flowing. "Who's there?"

"Michelle, silly. As we arranged."

Royston relaxed and opened the door.

Michelle threw her arms around him and hugged him tight. "Oh, Royston. Are you alright… it must have been terrifying." She stroked the back of his neck. "Have they found out who it was?" She let him go.

"No idea who it was. It all happened so quick, I didn't have time to take anything other than being strangled, on." He paused in painful reflection. "You think you can deal with anything, but… this was just so quick and well planned, I was powerless." His mind flashed back to his feeling of imminent death as the arm tightened around his neck. He shuddered. "I'm ok though, Michelle." He took her hand and walked over to the settee. "Would you like a drink while we look at the room service menu?"

"That sounds like a plan."

Royston opened the fridge and pulled out a bottle of champagne and two ice cold glasses that had been left by one of the stewards. "Is this OK?"

Michelle nodded. "Where are the menus?" She looked around, spotting them on the desk at the other side of the room. Royston grabbed them in passing as he placed the bottle and glasses in front of her on the glass coffee table.

"Here you are. See what's on offer." He opened the champagne and carefully poured two glasses, passing one over to her. "I am starving after losing my breakfast and lunch."

"Yuk. I don't need the gory details... thanks." She took her glass. "This is nice!"

Royston sipped at his glass. "It should be... It's Laurent Perrier." He looked through the menu. Some moments later and after re-reading the print, he sat back. "So, what are you having?"

"Simple... lobster starter, organic sea bass and raspberry pavlova. Probably a small portion of cheese and biscuits with a decent Stilton. What do you think for wine, Royston?"

"Hang on. I haven't got that far. First, I'll have same as you for starter, fillet steak with green peppercorn sauce and fruit salad to finish... and oh yes, cheese as well." He picked up the wine list and flicked through the pages. "I think we'll have a Chablis to start and then a Malbec after... if that's OK."

Michelle smiled. "Well, you're paying! I hope."

Royston raised his eyebrows. He ordered the meal over the phone and sat back next to Michelle.

She immediately laid back into his lap, snuggling down. "I was so scared you had been badly injured or worse. I just hope they catch the bastards... all the time they are at large, you're in danger and who knows who else will be caught up in it."

Royston stroked her neck. "Well, I don't know how this will pan out but I'd like to know why they picked me." He didn't want to say anything about the Jeffery Turner case, although he thought that this was at the heart of the attack. "The on-board security team seem to be on the ball, so I'll leave the investigating to them. I'll just keep a very keen eye on everything… " Royston sighed. "I was hoping to have a restful holiday. Some hope."

They fell silent, both happy to just sit and be quiet after the whirlwind last few hours. There was a knock at the door. Royston was immediately alert, his senses sharpened. Michelle sat up and Royston went cautiously across to the door, looked through the spy hole and noted that one of security guards he had seen earlier was standing there with the room service staff and a trolley of food. Royston opened the door and held it while the trolley was ceremoniously pushed into the room.

The main steward explained the various covered plates and dishes, while his colleague laid out the dining table. The two then left them to their food.

Both were ravenous and finished the meal in record time, only occasionally stopping to say how great the food tasted, washing the meal down with the excellent wines that they'd chosen.

Michelle sat back. "Phew. I'm full."

"Well, I definitely feel better with that lot inside me." He cleared the remnants back onto the trolley leaving the wine glasses on the table. Pushing the trolley carefully over to the door, he left it at one side.

Michelle collected the glasses and retired to the sofa. "I hope you are feeling better, Royston. I certainly am."

Royston joined her. "To be honest, although I was pretty shaken up, I don't seem to have had any long-term effects of the knock out drug. Maybe it'll hit me later." He stretched and put his arm round Michelle's shoulders.

She responded by snuggling up to him. "I feel safe with you, Royston." Looking up at him, she said quietly, "Maybe I should stay here tonight?"

"Well, that's a plan!" Royston reacted enthusiastically, too much so, he thought to himself. "I mean… that would be a good idea if it will make you feel safer."

"I think it's you who needs protecting." She smiled, sitting up. "I'll go and get some stuff. Be back shortly."

Thirty minutes later, she returned with an assortment of clothes, shoes and bags, which she unbundled onto one of the arm chairs.

"Are you thinking of moving in, Michelle?" Royston offered her some space in the wardrobe to hang her dresses up.

"That's a bit rude, Royston. I only want to look good for you!"

"Only joking. It's lovely to have you here." He back-tracked rapidly. "There's plenty of room and you really are welcome." He wrapped his arms round her. "You've been a real friend today… and more." They embraced.

Royston woke with a huge headache. At first, he didn't know where he was then sat up finding Michelle's arm across him. His brain snapped into gear… he remembered clearly the great night they had had together, the trials of the previous day forgotten in the passion of the night.

Rubbing his eyes to clear his sight, Royston fell out of bed and made for the shower. Ten minutes of flowing water sobered him up markedly. Emerging from the shower feeling at least partially alive, he kissed Michelle as their paths crossed.

She flashed a smile in reply. "Won't be long."

Royston dressed in casuals and looked at his watch... eight-thirty. He recognised that the gentle rolling of the ship had ceased and that they that they had already docked in Funchal. "Oh fuck." He was supposed to have been on deck one, helping the security staff look for the rogues who had robbed him. He called through to Michelle, having to shout above the sound of the power shower, "Stay here. I'll be back in an hour."

He dashed along the corridor to the lift lobby and impatiently pressed the lift button. Eventually one appeared and a minute later he arrived at deck one amid a general scrabble of passengers going ashore. Spying one of the security staff, he made his way across the deck to where he stood, checking the people as they tapped their ship ID cards on the wireless identifier. "Have you seen anything?" Royston instantly realised what a stupid question it was.

"No Mr. Fox," came the terse reply. "... and you standing here isn't going to make that any more likely. Go up to deck four under the life-tenders, where my colleague has been waiting for you. If you see anyone or anything that might help, let him know."

Royston felt like an idiot, really dressing himself down for yet again taking his eye off the ball. He ran up the stairs to the fourth deck and made his way outside and along to where he could see one the security staff leaning nonchalantly over the ship's railing.

"Ah, you made it then, Mr Fox. I'm Rick… security unit on board."

Royston felt the sarcastic barb in his tone. "Yes, sorry for being so late. I was feeling really rough actually, and only woke up late."

Rick gave an almost imperceptible shrug and returned his attention to the stream of people leaving the ship, and who were walking to the coaches which would take them into town. "Do you know what we are looking for?"

"The only clue I have is that two days ago I saw three guys in a private and obviously clandestine discussion in the Lido restaurant. They were talking to the Communications Officer who seemed to recognise me later… for no reason… when I went to the Purser's office. The other guys looked powerful men, not your regular cruise customer… but that could just be my imagination."

"Have you seen any of them since?" The guard continued to scrutinise the line of passengers.

"No. Not a sign of them… or at least none that I can remember." Just as Royston spoke, he saw the three men leave a group of passengers who had cleared the customs area and were now set to board the coaches. They broke the line and ran over to a waiting car parked next to the buses. "That's them. They're the guys I saw in the Lido…"

"Shit." Rick spoke loudly into his walkie talkie, but the car was already on its way and out of sight before he could ask for them to be stopped. He gave instructions for the car to be identified from the local cctv cameras. He told Royston that there was nothing more that could be done at this time, and that he should return to his cabin.

Royston actually felt relieved. At least the suspects had left the ship, or at least he assumed they had. He soon realised that any reduction in his anxiety was misplaced, as there could still be any number of accomplices still on board. By the time he arrived back at the cabin, his spirits were again low as he had realised that he actually still had no idea how all that had happened was connected, or indeed if it was connected

Michelle was still in the cabin, and seeing that Royston was looking decidedly down, she offered him a coffee. "So, what was that rush all about?"

"The security people wanted to see if I could identify any suspects over the mugging." He slumped on the sofa and laid back, eyes closed. And silent.

"And did you?" Michelle poured the hot water into the cup, handed him his coffee.

"I was late and the only people I suspected might be connected, got away before anything could be done."

Michelle handed him the coffee and kissed him on the forehead. "Well at least you're in one piece still."

Royston shrugged.

CHAPTER TEN

The two of them had decided to stay on board, if only to avoid exposing themselves to potential danger on shore. It proved to be a good decision as the sun was hot and the ship nearly empty. They enjoyed the quiet ambience of the swimming pool, jacuzzi and sun loungers, liberally interrupted by a waiter providing rehydration in the form of fruit cocktails.

The day passed well for them. The stress of the mugging and its aftermath at least seemed more distant. Michelle was tough but had never dealt with anything like this. Only with difficulty could she cast the previous day's happenings from her mind. She lay next to Royston and let her arm touch his. "Royston, do you think we should leave the ship and fly home?"

"I can't say I hadn't thought of that, but in all honesty, I feel less exposed here than I would at home… the two heavies have left the ship, and although there may be more, I actually doubt that. If they had wanted to do me in, they could have. I think this was much more an exercise in warning me off." He turned towards her. "I don't think anything else will happen here, and all bases are covered at home by my Met Police pal… so let's chill and enjoy the second half of the trip." He turned onto his back and felt the heat of the sun relax him.

For the first time on the cruise, Royston could truly relax and let his mind wander freely. He allowed himself to drift into a carefree zone, just enjoying a new feeling of peace. Two hours ticked by as Michelle and he dozed in the warm air. Royston sat up suddenly. "Why didn't they look at the CCTV footage from the mugging… they have cameras in all corridors?

Michelle had dozed off and woke with a start. "What?" She sat up and took a sip from her drink. "Sorry Royston, I didn't catch that."

"Why didn't they identify the muggers from the CCTV footage?"

Michelle shrugged. "Maybe there isn't any. Most systems have outages and downtime… or maybe they cut the cables or sprayed the lenses…."

Royston frowned. "But surely they have them all over the place… they must have caught them somewhere close or en-route or even leaving the vicinity."

"I can't answer that." She paused. "Maybe worth an enquiry though… go and see the Communications guy, especially as he was seen with the two men you suspect of doing the dirty deed."

"You've got a good point there. I'll call in after lunch and see what he says." Royston tensed up, thinking that there was a possibility of collusion between all of them, after all he had seen them huddled together in conversation. "Well, let's have some food and then I'll think about how to approach this."

They gathered their towels and other bits and pieces, and returned to the suite, changed and then headed for the Veranda restaurant.

An overly large lunch finished, Michelle returned to the suite while Royston wandered down to the purser's office to see if Mark Procter was available for a chat. A few minutes later, Royston was sitting outside the office waiting for the communications officer to emerge from his den, which he did so a few minutes later.

"Hello Mr Fox." He proffered his hand. "I hope you are recovering well and feeling much better."

Royston stood and took the man's hand. "Yes. I'm feeling a lot more sanguine about everything now, but must admit it was all a hell of a shock." They sat opposite one another.

"Can I get you a coffee or tea?"

"No thanks. I just dropped by to ask if any CCTV coverage had surfaced of the two suspects…." He paused waiting for a response.

Mark fidgeted in his chair. "Well actually we haven't any from your corridor. The camera was down at the time."

Royston seized the moment. "Well, how can that be? Surely, they must pass a number of them as they moved about the ship?"

"You are right. There are plenty of clips of them, but they were very clever and obviously well trained. Usually heads down as they passed key areas, or with peaked caps on. They were also not often, indeed seldom, seen together despite what you might have assumed." He fidgeted again. " Your cameras…one at either end of the corridor had both been subtly tampered with. They had their wires cut and reconnected. Very clever so that they could disconnect and re-connect at points someway from the cameras themselves and without being seen. So, the chances of being detected were slim and probably went unnoticed."

Royston felt irritation rising. "What you are saying is that they were able disconnect the cameras at will and then re-connect… all without being noticed. Surely the monitoring team should have been on the ball for such tampering?"

Mark coughed nervously. "Well actually, we do not have a fulltime monitoring team. It is all part of the on-board communications teams' duties. They have many other responsibilities. Quite often we rely on reviewing footage rather than monitoring." He paused. "But you must appreciate that staffing is tight."

Royston leant forward. "And what about the safety of the passengers? Don't they count, or is the policy 'money first' and bugger the punters, on this illustrious line?"

"Be fair, Mr Fox. No liners will have full time monitoring teams as we all have a range of duties. We have never had an incident like this which is a testament to our security. These two muggers were professionals who knew the system and exploited the loop holes well."

Royston felt that Procter was justifying the unjustifiable here. "I am very unhappy to hear that, Mr Procter, and I will be taking this up with the company when we get home."

"That's your prerogative, Mr Fox…" Procter looked uncomfortable. "But actually, I think you'll find that all of this is accepted practice on cruises." Again, he paused. "Not that that is any consolation, I agree… and I can't be sorrier about what has happened on my watch, believe me, Mr Fox. " He pursed his lips and frowned. "And…. I am going to be in the firing line when we dock in Southampton. But please be assured that I will be doing a very thorough job on the report. I will highlight all your comments to my security team on this ship and to the company senior advisors back home… I also expect you will also get some hefty compensation... and you have been upgraded to one of the best suites as well."

Before Royston could raise any objections, he jumped in again. "That of course is our obligation and pleasure, to help soothe the blow of being attacked on one of our flag ships."

Royston responded sharply. "Well, I would not expect anything less to be honest."

Mark looked down. "We'll send you copies of all relevant reports and communications, and when you're home please feel free to contact the shore team anytime. I'll give you full details before you disembark… and please be assured that we will do everything we can through all international crime agencies to bring these men to justice." He stood. "I have another meeting now, Mr. Fox so please accept my apologies for not staying longer. This is a busy time before we dock at Tenerife." He offered his hand.

Royston stood and took Mark's hand. "Well thanks for what you have been able to do. I do understand the difficulties and would really appreciate all the documentation you can give me. I'm going to follow it all up when I get home, and I know the police and insurance company will want sight of the documents as well."

Royston wandered up to the Lido restaurant and sent a text to Michelle to join him for a mid-afternoon tea. He sat there as he waited for a response, contemplating what Mark Procter had said. He understood the constraints, particularly if your opponents were clever, well briefed and determined, as these guys seemed to have been. He remembered his time in the Met when dealing with organised crime. No longer was it an issue of unintelligent crooks performing badly executed heists. It was more a game of hide and seek with highly organised and cunning gangs with huge resources, normally from the proceeds of drug dealing. There had been sea changes in the way crime needed to be fought.

Michelle broke into his revery. "Hi, lover boy… or should I say lover old boy." She laughed and ruffled his already messed up hair. She sat down with a bump next to him. "How did it go? Rubbish I expect."

"Well, you are partly right. Mark Procter was actually sympathetic and honest. He said they CCTV had been spiked and they had no useful footage so far." He stood. "What do you want to drink, Michelle?"

"Oh. I'll have a hot chocolate please."

Royston wandered over to the array of drinks dispensers and poured a coffee and a hot chocolate. The ship responded to a slight swell with a sudden judder, nearly making him spill the liquid. He regained balance as the side thrusters equilibrated the vessel. "Oops. Nearly lost the lot there." He handed Michelle her drink and carefully placed his on the table and sat down. "That's the first lurch I've experienced on this trip."

"Thanks." She slurped her drink, the froth arranging itself in an arc along her top lip. She laughed and licked it carefully away. "I was thinking, Royston… I think That we could do a bit of internet trawling for key facts of what has happened. You know, see if any of it has happened and been reported before. I have access to some sites which you would not have… through my work in security. I may well be able to find out if what has happened is part of something bigger or more widespread."

"Yeah." Royston cupped his mug of coffee between his hands and rested his elbows on the table. "This whole saga must be part of something bigger… we can't see it yet, but I think I am beginning to sense something much wider than a simple lost person here. Especially with Turner dead and no sign of his wife… and of course the attack on me…" He trailed off, thinking of how it was all linked.

We aren't going to discover anything unless we pool resources and dig deep. Let's have a look at some stuff before dinner. We can go to the library… nice and private there, but still in full sight so to speak."

Royston smiled. "Good idea. But first I am going to have some cake… there's a tray of all sorts up there at the moment. I need an energy boost."

They finished their tea with two slices of cake each, plus a small Danish pastry. Arm in arm they made their way down to deck three and into the upper floor of the library. There was no-one else there so they were able to take their pick of desks, choosing one that overlooked the sea through a large window. The sun shone and all was well.

CHAPTER ELEVEN

Michelle made herself comfortable in front of the computer, with Royston sat at her side. They had decided on this arrangement as Michelle was much faster at keyboard input, and Royston wanted to have thinking time as they started entering questions or looking for information.

They had decided that they should delve as deeply as possible into Jeffery Turner's wife's details and see if they could elicit any new information. As Turner himself was dead, the wife might be the only connection to whatever was going on. Royston realised that she might indeed have been done in herself, and that they may never find any information, but it seemed the right place to start.

"Let's bring up all possible details about her…I'll start with my genealogy site." She typed in Sarah Elizabeth Todd and waited. A string of names filled the screen. "Mmm. Quite a popular name over the years." She quickly ran the cursor over the list on the front page and then onto the next two pages. "What was her D.O.B.?"

Royston looked at his notes. "Twentieth of October nineteen seventy-three. Is she there?"

Michelle again reviewed the list. Well, there's a Sarah Juliette Elizabeth Todd with that birthday. That must be her. She was born in Chatham and had what looks like a normal parentage… both mum and dad listed as married and working. All looks normal to me. I suggest you note her parent's address, as many people end up living where their parents had been."

Royston dutifully copied the family address. It was sometimes useful delving into the parent's details; where they lived, what was their local hospital and what church they got married in, again because all connections remained relevant until found to be useless. A picture of an ordinary middle-class family was emerging, at this stage with no contact to the marine life of Jeffery Turner.

"Let's find their marriage details if they are there."

Michelle quickly moved registers and typed in the names. Again, a long list of marriages emerged. She quickly eliminated the irrelevant and focused on one set of details. "This is it, Royston. Jeffery Michael Turner married to Sarah Juliette Elizabeth Todd, married on the twenty-ninth of July twenty oh three."

Royston scribbled the date down. "…and where?"

Michelle squinted at the screen. "St. Williams' Church in Waldersdale Road, Chatham. Looks like a normal sort of CofE affair. Witnesses were Sarah's dad and one of Jeffery's mates… a Frederick Bedford."

Royston again noted the details down. "Can we see if they had any kids?"

Michelle nodded and again switched registers. After a lot of typing and scrutiny of lists, they both agreed that there were no children involved. "I'll dig into that a bit deeper when we've got more time, but it looks as if they were married for about twenty years and had no kids."

Something was niggling at Royston's brain. He couldn't pinpoint it. "There's something in all that, that is pinging in my brain but I can't pinpoint it. I'll let it stew for a bit and see what my head comes up with later."

It all looks ordinary and normal to me, Royston…." She closed the marriage section. Let's have a look at my people search that I use when looking for baddies on the internet." She keyed in some requests faster than Royston could follow. "I've asked for connections between all the names we've found so far. It'll take a few minutes to regurgitate anything it's found." Michelle arched back in her chair and stretched her legs. "Isn't the sea beautiful in the sun?"

Royston had to agree. The simple colours and shades of the scene from their window could be anywhere in the world, but the constantly changing surges and splashes of the near calm sea, presented an ever-changing scene of infinite shades in deep blue.

Michelle looked back at the screen. She frowned. "It's saying here that the information is sensitive and cannot be viewed without clearance from the site owner." She paused. "But we own the site, or at least me and my business partners own it… so why can't I see the info with my top end clearance." She was genuinely puzzled. "That's never come up before. I need to speak to my partners back home. I'll send him an encrypted message… now."

Clearly concerned, Michelle drafted a quick but to the point message and pinged it off to her partners. They waited. A message came back. She leant forward. "Now let's see what they say…" She read the brief message. "They say that someone in the list is on the National Security watchlist and details are guarded by MI6. No way round it, we can't access the info."

Royston had thought through the data they had seen online. "The only connection with anything untoward in what we've dug up, is that Jeffery Turner was being watched by the security people, but now he's dead surely everything else is OK for us to investigate."

"Obviously not. Maybe someone else is on the hot list…. Not just Jeffery himself." Is it possible one of the parents or his wife's connections are also dodgy?" Michelle closed the messaging system and returned to the main screen.

Royston thought for a moment. "Run through the names again, Michelle."

"You've written them down yourself, dafty." She smiled to relieve the tension.

"Oh, yes. Silly me...." Royston checked his paperwork. "Not much here." He rubbed his forehead and frowned. "The only slight connection might be the witness to their marriage... Frederick Bedford... Jonathan Bedford was the intelligence guy I met with Mike McCarthy, but that really is grasping at straws."

"That sounds a bit far fetched, Royston, I agree. What else is tweaking your 'little grey cells'?"

Royston puffed his cheeks and breathed out. "Haven't got an f'ing clue, Michelle. We're getting nowhere... How about delving into his wife's background. you know, friends, contacts work etcetera. Maybe that's the way in?"

Michelle started a new search. "Worth a try."

Royston stayed silent as she typed and waited, typed and waited, and again. "Anything coming up?"

Michelle leant back again. "Well, here's something. It appears Sarah, despite her very English name, appears to have been born and brought up in Leipzig... in Germany, not in Chatham. She started out as Lotte Elisabet Todt... easy to change to her current ID."

Royston's interest was pricked. "That means she was East German, part of the old communist regime. The Berlin wall only came down in 1991 which makes her twentyish when that happened. She must have been one of the young either sympathisers or rebels."

Royston sat up and leant closer to the screen. "let's see where an enquiry on that line goes?"

Michelle's attention was now fully on the job at hand. "I think I can access the old East German archives. Most remained intact and can now be looked at on-line… in a spirit of unification and as a warning as to just how bad things were then."

They both sat focused on the flashing screen as Michelle accessed page after page of data… lists and lists of names, dates and notes." I never realised just how pervasive those bastards were. It looks as if every household had an informer who was part of the close family. Communism was an appalling philosophy in practice, clothed in a cloak of equality. I'm amazed that people were taken in, but then again, we nearly ended up with an extreme left-wing government in Britain ourselves, recently. People have short memories…"

Royston suddenly pointed at the screen. "Look. That's her! What does it say?"

Michelle stared intensely at the screen. "Well, that is interesting… she was a member of the young communists and became an informer in her group… even informing on her family by the looks of it. She was employed by the Stasi and was moving up the ranks when the regime imploded. The records just stop with no info on where she went, but… it looks as if she was trained to be an infiltrator, even a spy. But this would all have to be cross-referenced with the Stasis's files which are not so freely available."

"Does your company have access to that sort of thing?" Royston's brain was working overtime. "If we could find out what happened next, I think we will be able to see the bigger picture and why everything has escalated as it has."

Michelle shook her hands to return the circulation to normal. "My hands are going numb!" She circled her shoulders to loosen them up. "Not as easy as that Royston. I suspect we will have been watched remotely… even now and even through an encrypted link. Remember you got hacked last time we tried to investigate. I think after what has happened, our every move will have been clocked and we'll probably soon see a response, even if it is to simply shut us down, as before."

Royston gently thumped the arm of his chair with his fist. "That's bloody ridiculous. Especially as all this info is freely available on line."

"Not quite freely. Our government, the US, NATO, the EU and Russia… and probably China are all still looking at these historic links with communism and terror. It is well known that the terrifying KGB and Stasi did not simply give up when the Berlin Wall fell. They simply retreated back into the shadows. While everyone was congratulating themselves on flattening Communism, the secret services in those countries were re-organising and smarting from having their perks removed and power apparently gone, eager for revenge. Just look at Putin's world to see how wrong we all were." Michelle smiled.

"Oops. Sorry for the rant. Time for a cocktail I think!"

Royston exhaled loudly. "You're not wrong there. I'll think it all through and start a detailed Gantt chart to try to establish and follow the links and connections that we've unearthed so far."

Michelle logged off and stood, stretching as she did so. "Sitting like that always makes me stiff."

"Agreed. Let's retire to the Golden Lion for some lubrication."

Michelle caught his hand as they made their way along the corridor to the Pub on that deck. "I hope I'm helping you, Royston. I don't want there to be any more trouble."

Royston tightened his grip on her hand. "I don't think I would be in such good shape without you here, so don't worry. I couldn't do without you." He pulled her close. "You've been fantastic."

She blushed. "Well, I wouldn't be anywhere else but with you." She looked down, slightly embarrassed by her sentiment.

Entering the pub, they picked a table again looking out to sea. Ordering two cocktails, they sat in silence, allowing the ship's gentle movement to settle them. Royston supped his drink. "That's better. Where do you think we should eat this evening. There's a good show on, so if we eat early, we can see the later performance."

"That's fine with me, Royston".

CHAPTER TWELVE

Royston and Michelle had had a little too much to drink that evening, with a fun time in the Golden Lion pub testing the beers, followed by a super dinner with an overly expensive but perfect wine. This was followed by a night cap in the Commodore's Club and then a collapse into bed, having missed the entertainment.

Michelle awoke with the thud of the liner being docked in Tenerife, the biggest of the Islands and a very popular haunt and favourite of the British. It was early…three thirty. She looked over at Royston who was still asleep and buried in the voluminous duvet. Michelle considered waking him, but discretion won. Pouring herself a glass of water she returned to bed with the latest novel in her reading list. She hadn't got very far with that, as her teaming up with Royston hadn't been on her itinerary when she left Southampton.

Within half an hour she was back asleep only to be woken by Royston, two hours later as he tumbled out of bed with a loud curse. Startled, she opened her eyes to Royston hopping about, swearing at his bruised toes which had made contact with the bed base as he wobbled to the loo.

He sat on the end of the bed nursing his foot. "Ouch…ouch…ouch." He exhaled loudly. "That was bloody painful."

Michelle offered some ice.

"No thanks. The bones will knit together in six weeks or so." Eventually he disappeared into the bathroom and Michelle settled back into the warmth of the bed.

He emerged some while later, a little more sanguine. He dried his hair vigorously with a large towel. "That's better. I feel a bit more human after that shower. Must have washed out some of the alcohol."

Michelle laughed. "You still don't look that good… I'll have a shower now." She slipped out of bed and made her way to the bathroom under Royston's admiring eye. "See you in a bit."

Royston knew from brief experience that this meant he could probably go for breakfast, come back and read a book before she emerged. He smiled. "OK."

Royston wrapped the large towel around his midriff and opened the balcony door. Stepping out into the morning air, he rested on the rail of the cabin which was on the water side of the dock. The weather was superb, blue cloudless sky, blue seas and no swell of any significance. The bustle of the shore crew was audible in the still morning air and the vague smell of diesel from the pilots' tugs which were fussing around the front of the ship, lingered in the air.

He closed his eyes and rotated his shoulders which were still stiff and achy after the stress of the last few days. He determined to go for a therapeutic massage to iron out his tired muscles. He dressed and made a cup of coffee. He watched the news and browsed the leaflet detailing the day's activities on and off board. The trip to Mount Teide appealed to him, as although he had been to this island before, he had never taken the cable car to the top of the massive central peak. It was a long trip from the South of the island up through foothills, through the sparce forest and over into the caldera of the volcano. That rim was the furthest he had been on previous trips, and now he felt, was the time to go the whole hog.

As he mused on the possibilities, Michelle emerged from the shower, wrapped up in a myriad of towels and wearing a turban around her hair. "Phew. That was nice." She unfurled the towel on her head and shook to loosen her hair.

Royston just looked. She really was a beautiful woman. He nodded his head imperceptibly as if acknowledging just how lucky he was to have encountered her on this voyage. "I thought we'd take the trip to the top of Mount Teide today, if you'd like to?"

She screwed up her face. "Not sure about that. Isn't it long old way… and a cable car…" Her voice trailed off.

Royston didn't want to force her, but company would be good. "I'll look after you!" He smiled. "I'll make sure you don't fall out of the cable car."

Michelle started dressing. "I suppose it would be fun. I've never been up there." She pulled on a baggy pair of flower bespattered shorts. "We've probably missed the booking time now. Why don't you give the purser's office a ring and see?"

"Good idea. Better still I'll go down and see if we can book a couple of places." He left her finishing off her beautification process.

He took the lift to the first floor and went over to the desk. There were only a couple of people ahead of him and he rapidly arrived at the front of the queue such as it was. "Have you still got any places on the Mount Teide trip?"

"Sorry sir that went an hour ago. It's a long trip and we need to make sure everyone arrives back in good time to sail this evening."

Royston was a bit crestfallen. "Well, can we go by taxi?"

"That's a possibility sir, but you will have to back by five thirty this evening. From here it's about a two- and half-hour trip there and back. I can arrange a taxi for you if you would like?"

Royston wasn't sure. "Oh, what the heck. Yes, can you order one for us to pick up the quay terminal here?" I'll go and get my partner and we can go in about half an hour."

"What is your state room number sir?"

Royston had to think as he was now in a different area of the ship. "Err… Oh yes the Caronia Suite.

Deck seven… err…seven, oh, eight, five." He felt embarrassed as he didn't feel like a grand suite sort of person. Not that he was complaining.

That revelation brought the steward at the desk up with a visible jolt. "Ah. Fine sir I'll do that immediately and speak to your personal suite steward with all the details. Would you like us to organise a personal guide?"

Royston was now embarrassed at all the fussing. "No. No that'll be fine just make sure we can fit the visit in easily enough. Don't want to miss the ship."

"Right sir. I'll get onto that straight away."

Royston was happy to escape and made his way back to the suite. He let himself in and sat heavily on the sofa. "Well, that was an eye-opener. Everything was fine until I have my room number. Then it was all, rather obsequious… not to my liking at all."

Michelle smiled. "That's what you get for being a top bod on such a ship. They don't much care unless you've oodles of dosh, and having a suite like this signifies just that. They're now going to expect a big tip." She sat down next to him and nuzzled his neck. "I might even like you a bit better now!"

There was a buzz at the door. Michelle opened the door after checking through the spy hole.

"Is Mr Fox there, madam?".

Royston came to the door.

"Here are your travel arrangements for Mount Teide, sir." He handed over a neat folder of papers. "Everything is there, sir. The taxi is waiting at the terminal security gate and the driver has been instructed to take you where you want to go… and of course all paid for by Cunard." He nodded. "Enjoy, sir."

Michelle was taken aback. "Good grief. They really are worried you'll give them bad publicity. Still, enjoy it while you…and I of course…can. I think we should grab some food from the Lido to take with us. I'm already hungry."

"Good idea." Royston too, was feeling more than peckish.

They made their way to the ships exit via the restaurant. They explained to one of the floor managers what they wanted, and again everything was laid on for them. They were given a veritable feast for their day and wished well on their way.

"I could get used to this service, Royston. Can I come with you next trip?" She smiled and tugged him closer as they walked down the interminable zig-zag gang plank which more resembled the walk to an airport terminal than to the quayside. Eventually they arrived at ground level and out into the warm air. Passports were checked and they were waved on into the port Santa Cruz de Tenerife. Royston looked around and saw a taxi driver with a card with his name on it lofted, so that it could be seen above the rest of the people milling around.

The driver was a very pleasant Spaniard, and drove a rather large Mercedes. They both piled into the back seat which had plenty of room for far bigger people than they. Royston explained what they wanted and it seemed that everything had been organised already. "It's a long drive, sir, so make yourself comfortable and enjoy the ride."

The journey was indeed a long one, but Tenerife is a very varied island with many different and interesting villages and views which made the time pass quickly. They drove through the Teide National Park and towards the towering peak of the huge volcano. It became even more impressive as you moved closer. They arrived at what looked like a tourist centre with a restaurant and other facilities close by, and a cable car terminal prominent and towering with the wires visible right up the side of the volcano.

The taxi driver asked for their tickets, took them and walked past the large snaking queue of tourists obviously waiting to buy passes and board the cable car. He spoke to what looked like a supervisor and Royston and Michelle were ushered through a separate door and directly onto the waiting cable car. "I'll be here when you come back down Sir. Here's my card. If you can, give me a call when you are leaving the top." He paused and smiled. "Enjoy."

Michelle held Royston tight as the glass enclosed carriage looped its way up towards the top of Teide. She wasn't going to show that she was scared, and neither was Royston. They passed through a thin cloud layer which presented an amazing change of view as though they were suddenly in an aircraft looking down from the sky onto the clouds. The final few metres into the arms of the top cable car station, was the most traumatic with the car swaying as it came to a halt. It seemed very strange stepping out onto solid land.

The air was thin and they both caught their breath as their breathing caught up with the lack of oxygen. Teide was three and half thousand metres at its peak and the air was thin, catching the unwary who had not experienced that atmosphere before.

"That is weird, Royston. I had not realised just how much this altitude would affect my breathing." Michelle steadied herself against Royston, who had to admit even he was struggling to adapt. They made their way out of the terminal and quickly found a seat to rest on. They sat, and neither talked. The scenery was breath-taking. They could see the coast and the slope of the mountain fading in perspective to the azure sea.

"That is an amazing view, Royston." She rested her head on his shoulder. "I'm so glad you thought of this. I would never have come on my own."

Royston stroked her hair. "Well, I'm pleased to be sharing it with you. When you're ready we'll take a short stroll along the view path. We have to stay on that as no-one is now allowed to ascend to the summit... apparently people were starting to damage the ground leading up to the peak." He paused. "I don't want to go any higher anyway."

"Nor me."

After ten minutes they laboriously made their way along one of the available paths to a viewpoint where the view was again spectacular. Royston paused and leant on a hand rail, looking around at the view.

Suddenly he stiffened. "Shit." He tugged Michelle's arm and spun her back round to face the terminal. Put your hood up and do not show your face."

She obliged. "What on earth's the matter?"

Royston wrapped his head tightly in the hood of his jacket. "It's those two bastards that attacked me. They must be here looking for me. I don't want to meet them up here."

CHAPTER THIRTEEN.

Royston was now in full emergency mode. "Right Michelle, we're getting back to the taxi asap. Keep your hood up and look down. We'll not do anything to draw attention, and make our way casually to the Cable car."

They moved with another group of tourists along the path back to the building. Royston discreetly looked around for the two men. They were not to be seen. Entering the cable car cabin, Michelle nudged Royston. "They're over there she whispered over by the building entrance. Royston shuffled to the far end of the cabin and set himself in a defensive position able to cover all angles of view if the men entered. His heart was thumping with adrenalin. Glancing up he saw the men step in through the door. They didn't seem to notice Royston.

The cable car left its dock and swung out into open air. Neither Royston or the men moved. He could feel Michelle shudder next to him. He gently squeezed her hand in a reassuring way, although he didn't feel that secure himself despite there being twenty people in the cabin. The journey seemed to take an eternity.

As they neared the start point, Royston carefully surveyed the area for their taxi. He hadn't had time to make contact. He quickly sent a text message and saw their driver head for the taxi as the cable car arrived. The cabin emptied and the two men left without apparently noticing Royston and Michelle some way behind them.

"Keep your head down, Michelle and don't rush. Follow me." Royston guided her firmly towards their waiting vehicle in the car park. He opened the door. "Get in quickly." He unceremoniously shoved her into the back of the car and jumped in after her. As he did this, he saw the two men running towards them, not far distant. "Leave quickly please driver… we've got some unwanted company."

Just as the car pulled away, there was a heavy thump on the window next to Michelle. One of the men had hit the window with some object which looked like the butt of a gun.

"Christ, get a move on, man." Royston flicked the door locks to make sure they were secure. "They mean business."

As they left the car park, the two men clambered into their own car, a large black Mercedes, and gunned the engine into action. A cloud of dust and gravel flew into the air drawing attention to their rapid exit.

The taxi only had a few hundred metres lead. Royston turned his head to look back at their pursuers. "I hope you are a good driver… we are being followed and the men in the Mercedes won't take prisoners."

Luckily for you Mr Fox., I am an ex-police driver from Spain. We are trained well. So, if he tries anything I think I can cope."

Royston was surprised. "That's reassuring." He turned to Michelle. "Make sure your belt is secure, and hold onto me if things get rough."

"Actually, Mr Fox., I'm part of the detail attached to the ship's security. I know what's been happening and we were prepared for this. We had been tipped off that the two heavies had moved ahead to Tenerife. We have good links with the Canarian mafia informants… they keep their ears to the ground when we need them. The Canaries are an international intelligence base for many nations, but particularly Europe, East and West. Comes in handy some times." The car swerved as it was thumped from behind by the Mercedes. "Tighten your belts…we're in for a fight."

The roads of the National Park ran through an area of volcanic sand and pumice which formed a very dangerous surface if you happened to be pushed off the road. The Mercedes hit again.

"Hold on… I'm going to keep him at bay with speed if I can, until we start up the caldera wall." Luckily cars were few and far between either way. They had to slow at one point because there were three cars in front all pootling along enjoying the view. Their driver slammed the car into third, keeping the revs high ready to accelerate into an overtake. The Mercedes tried to pass but the police driver nudged him out towards the rough stopping the manoeuvre in its tracks… they tried the other side with the same result. Just as the car following had to duck back in behind, Royston's car accelerated around the slow traffic and gained some valuable distance which he was able to maintain for some way.

Within a few kilometres the black car was back harrowing the tail of their own vehicle. Several times it swerved one way or the other, to try and shove the taxi or overtake. The police driver was good. He parried all attempts to get by or make the car swerve off the road and kept them safe from all attempts to knock them off course. Again and again the danger was averted… other cars on the road were used as a shield to prevent attacks, but once the Mercedes edged close to being able to push past, but luckily an on-coming lorry prevented this happening. The two cars accelerated together up the first section slop onto a level narrow and twisting section.

Michelle whispered to Royston that she was feeling very sick. He just held her close.

"All set?" Royston wondered who the driver was talking to. Before he could ask, the single word "affirmative" came back over the radio.

"Who was that?" Royston queried.

"The base team. Sit tight, this could be a bit scary." The Mercedes was now gaining on them as they approached the second climb towards the caldera rim. "Get ready."

Michelle and Royston braced themselves for who knew what. Their car slowed and Royston could see the car following hitting the breaks with cloud of smoke erupting from the rear, as they tried to avoid crashing into the back. Just when a collision looked inevitable, the police driver accelerated at maximum creating quite a gap between the two cars before the Mercedes could react. Just as this gap appeared, so too did a pair of uniformed men sling two 'stingers' between the cars. The steely spikes glistened in the sun as the black car approached.

Royston looked back through the rear window. The Mercedes hit the first stinger and swerved but kept control. Not so when it hit the second. The black car reared up and flew through the air rotating gracefully as it plunged to a near immediate and shuddering halt, embedded in a wall of volcanic rock.

"Bloody hell…" Royston was shocked. Their car slowed to a halt in a lay by some distance from the crash.

The driver looked back. "Stupid men. I don't think you'll be seeing any more of them on this journey, Mr Fox."

The embedded car burst into flames. No-one got out and only a small group of uniformed men looked on at a distance.

Michelle was shaking. Royston was not much better but held her close. Taking a deep breath, he gathered his thoughts. Despite the hair-raising chase they had just been part of, he actually felt safe. At least the danger was over for the moment.

Their driver started the car and set off up the road towards Santa Cruz de Tenerife. "We'll get you back to the ship and I'm sure our security people will want to debrief you."

The journey back passed in silence. Michelle fell asleep and Royston just sat and mused on where the whole Jeffery Turner saga was heading. He had honestly felt that the two heavies leaving the ship a few days back, was the end of the story, at least until he had returned home. He couldn't really see why they were still after him. He had no direct involvement with the truth of the case, rather, his was a peripheral role almost as a bystander.

Mentally retracing his steps, he could not think of anything that would necessitate his death or that of Michelle. As he backtracked again, he decided that the only link to anything even remotely unsettling was the East German connection they had only just discovered. Royston knew quite a lot about the Iron Curtain Countries as he had lived through the end of that nightmare. If the communist extremists were rearing their ugly heads again, he was sure he did not want to become entangled.

He was miles away when the car turned into the dock car park and stopped near a group of serious looking security staff. The car door was opened and the woman who was obviously the top bod asked him to follow her. Michelle and he were whisked away to a bleak office in the customs building and seated in cold plastic chairs at an oblong table in the centre of the room. Guards were posted outside and inside the door and the woman sat down opposite them.

Her English was immaculate. "I am Constantine Marar, Mr Fox, from Spanish intelligence." She looked him straight in the eyes. "You are now directly connected with three deaths, one in the United Kingdom and two here on Tenerife. We have found your traces all over the trail from England to the ship and now to here." She paused and flicked through a thick folder of papers and photographs. "We have spoken to the British police… a Michael McCarthy… and also the MI5 and MI6 contacts we have, and they have marked you out as the connection between the death of Jeffery Turner, the mugging on the ship and now the car chase ending in the deaths of the two men we needed to interrogate as a link to whoever it is chasing you." She spread her hands that were resting on the table, inviting a response.

Royston paused. "Well, none of that is news, is it. I have been chased, mugged and nearly killed… it is obviously not me you should be interrogating… or Michelle here." Royston had decided on a positive but challenging response to this questioning. "We have been scared stiff by the mounting threats that have followed us from one place to another. We have obviously tried to find out what was going on, and the only important connection seems to be with

Turner's wife… which is how all this started. She was my entry point into this mystery."

"I'm listening." Constantine scribbled briefly on her notepad. " Go on…"

"I found no trace of her at home. We tried again yesterday on-line and with a bit of lateral thinking found out that she was a Stasi agent from old East Germany, in the bad old days of the Iron Curtain. She changed her name and then decamped to the UK, apparently concealing the change… as you would. She did officially marry Jeffery under the changed name of Sarah Todd. That's where the trail ends and all we know at the moment."

Constantine raised her eyebrows slightly. "Impressive… but of course we know all that, as do British intelligence. To add to it, we know she made a bee-line for Jeffery Turner as soon as she'd been allowed to come to the UK, and that they had paired up as an espionage team… for the US. That's the only way she could have escaped scrutiny when she went the to UK… her past must have been hidden at some official level. British intelligence only became aware of them after a few years of activity. Then everything went quiet and they faded from the radar… until now." She closed her file. "I think you've probably had enough for one day. We think the danger for you has passed, at least until you get home. I suggest you do not leave the ship until you reach Southampton, as we cannot guarantee your safety if you wander off on your own again." She stood and clasped her file under an arm. "We'll send a report to MI6 and I'm sure they will want to speak to you when you get home, at some point."

Royston eased out of his chair and helped Michelle to her feet. She was still shaking visibly. "We're going to get checked out by the ship's medical team, have some food and then crash out for a bit. We're very much in need of some quiet." He glanced at Michelle who was pale and shaken.

Constantine nodded to the security guards by the door. "They will escort you back on-board and give you an emergency communicator that will summon help very quickly if you need it. Thank you for your assistance. Rest assured we will be watching." She shook Royston and Michelle's hands and left with her team.

CHAPTER FOURTEEN.

Royston fumbled with his room key card, eventually unlocking the door. He let Michelle through and followed her into their suite. Michelle burst into tears, no longer able to hide her emotions. Royston held her close and stroked her hair. "We're luckily in one piece. We're not taking any more risks…. none. These bastards are clearly more dangerous than we thought. It is so lucky that the police and security were on the ball. If we had had an ordinary taxi driver, I am sure we would have been dead or seriously injured now."

Michelle had stopped sobbing and was now just breathing in gulps. "I thought we were going to die, Royston… that was so scary."

"Royston guided her over to the bed. We're going to shower get dressed up and have a bumper room service dinner… here… with no-one else around."

Michelle gathered a change of clothes and went into the shower room. She was slowly feeling more settled. "I'll clean up and be out in a few minutes."

Royston sat heavily on the sofa having made himself a coffee. He had to admit to himself that he had nearly cracked up during the car chase and had wanted to stop and face up to the thugs. That fleeting thought had passed, luckily, and he had steeled himself for whatever happened. He now felt completely drained and flat. Contemplating calling

Mike McCarthy, he eventually decided a brief text would be better as he didn't feel up to a long explanatory conversation. He asked Mike to give him a call in the morning. Sitting back, he closed his eyes and almost immediately drifted off.

The next he knew was a gentle prod from Michelle who was standing in front of him, wrapped in a towel. "Are you O.K. Royston?"

Waking with a start, he carefully stretched his neck which had obviously been lolling in a fixed awkward position. "Ouch."

Michelle stood behind him and gently massaged the offending muscles. "Does that help?"

"Absolutely... Carry on... or perhaps not, or I'll go back to sleep." Again, he stretched his neck and shoulders. "That's great. You look better yourself... how do you feel? Less anxious I hope." He stood and drew her to him, kissing her on the forehead. "You seem better than you did when we got back here." He held her tight for a few moments. "I'll get showered and we'll order up some food for later, and have a drink to relax us."

Grabbing some clothes, he spread them on the bed and went into the shower room. "I'll be awhile, love. I need to wash the brickbats out." He realised he had called her 'love'. It felt natural.

In the shower he let the water cascade over him, relaxing, he tried to clear his mind. Not an easy task he found. After several minutes he could feel his shoulders easing and the tensions start to ebb. He realised that yet again he had underestimated the unseen opposition and determined himself never to repeat that near fatal mistake. Thinking through the day, he realised that if he had been on the alert, he would have sensed the coming problems simply by opening his eyes and looking around earlier. Clearly the security team had known and he wondered why they hadn't warned him. Perhaps they thought that an undercover police driver would be enough. Royston was puzzled, as it seemed that Michelle and he had been deliberately and unknowingly exposed to huge danger which could have been avoided.

It seemed to him that they had been used as bait to catch the two marauding heavies that they had so spectacularly missed earlier in the week. Royston felt quite angry and thought he might ask some questions. It was then that he realised that he had no names or phone numbers to speak to anyone. All he had was the alarm dongle given to him by Constantine. The security guy on the door was a member of the ship's team so probably didn't know anything. Deciding the questions would have to wait, he turned the shower off, dried himself and returned to the main room.

Michelle looked fabulous. "I'd better get my glad rags on, I see."

She smiled. "You look like a wild man… your hair is all standing on end… and the towel doesn't do you any favours." She poured two large brandies as he pulled on his clothes.

"God, I feel as if I've been kicked in the back." He was having trouble reaching far enough down to pull on his socks. Grimacing with the pain in his back, eventually he managed the task. "I think we're both going to feel it tomorrow... if my backs tweaking now, tomorrow should be fun!". He arched his back several times to loosen it up. "A couple of brandies should help."

Clinking glasses they sat at the table and looked through the room-service a la carte menu. Royston glanced at his watch. "It's near half five. A bit early for dinner. What time do you want to eat?"

"Five minutes ago." She laughed. "I'm ravenous. We missed lunch and I haven't eaten anything since early this morning."

"You've recovered well. OK, what are you choosing." Choosing their food slowly and their wine even slower, Royston eventually called through to room-service and ordered. "They say the food will be about forty minutes and would we like the wine now?" He looked at Michelle.

"Let's have it now."

Putting the phone down, Royston returned to the sofa and took up his glass. "We'd better finish this then." He gulped down the not small brandy and replaced the glass on the table. "That went down well."

Michelle was more circumspect and sipped her drink. After a few minutes the door buzzer sounded. Royston went to the door and checked who it was, and recognising their steward, he opened the door.

Two bottles of wine on a tray were placed on the sideboard with four glasses. Two for the white wine they had chosen and two for the red. "Would you like me to open the wine, sir? The red will need to breathe, so I am presuming you would like the white first as an apéritif.

"That'd be fine, thanks."

After the steward had skilfully opened the wines, one, a light golden French Gavi, and the other a deep red and rich Malbec, both favourite wines of theirs. He poured a sip of Gavi into one of the glasses and handed it to Royston who swirled it around, peered at it and then carefully downed the liquid, savouring the flavour in his mouth and throat. "That tastes lovely." He never really knew how to respond on such occasions and always felt self-conscious performing that little ritual associated with wine tasting.

Pouring two fuller glasses of the light-yellow liquid, the steward replaced the bottle on the tray and retreated, closing the door almost silently as though not wishing to disturb the quiet.

Michelle and Royston sat in silence and enjoyed the wine, neither feeling it necessary to speak. They had both been on the edge of terror, and now felt words would not add to this moment of recovery. Michelle broke their revery. "Do you want a fill up?" She stood and collected the wine bottle.

Royston realised he had been lost in thought and also absently had emptied his glass. "That'd be nice. I might even taste this one."

Michelle smiled and refilled his glass. Topping up her own, she sat on the sofa and nudged up to him. "I feel safe with you."

A short while later their food arrived. The smell made them realise just how hungry they were. There were no scraps left at the end of the meal and both were feeling full and better for the replacement of energy. Finishing off the wine, Royston placed the tray outside the door.

"I presume you don't want to go to the show this evening?" Turning to Michelle he saw that she had spread herself along the sofa.

"No. I want to stay here… with you."

Royston sat down on the edge. "I'm knackered too. An early night, I think. Before that though, I do want to see how we access the historic Stasi files… hopefully online."

Michelle sat upright, frowning. "That's romantic then," she responded with slight sarcasm,

Tugging him towards her, she kissed him. "I suppose I can wait until you've finished."

Opening up and booting the laptop, Royston positioned his notepaper on his right. "Where shall we start?"

"Well first by connecting via the advanced VPN network… that should keep us safe from prying eyes… and second make sure you do not accept any cookies." She nudged him out of the way, reaching across to input her choices. "In fact, if you use DuckDuckGo browser and search engine, we'll be pretty safe."

Royston looked at her quizzically. "Why not use your company network? You said it was completely hack proof."

She made herself more comfortable by his side. "I thought we would, and then on second thoughts, it might flag us up and allow any nasties to put two and two together… the network and our position, if they were randomly scanning our searches."

"Surely a VPN will not allow them to track our location."

"You would think so wouldn't you, but these security agencies have phenomenal powers at their disposal, and sometimes simplicity creates less waves over the Internet. Sometimes being obvious means that no-one bothers looking at your presence. So, I suggest we do what millions of others are doing, rather than try to be too clever… less chance of being flagged up I think."

"OK Michelle. You're the expert. Let's kick off by doing a general enquiry… 'where are the Stasi files'… that'll give us a starting point." He typed in the question.

They both squinted at the listed responses. Royston pointed to one. "That looks like the official archives… let's try that." Clicking on the link, the German official archives screen appeared. "There's everything there, but we won't be able to access it because we are not relatives and media and research requests take days to agree."

"OK. Let's look at some of the lower ones…" Royston scrolled slowly down the list. They looked at many websites, but nothing stood out as being interesting. "I think this was a bad idea, Michelle." He stretched back and loosened his shoulders. "This woman Todt, is not on public view… as I found out when doing my original searches."

Michelle loosened her neck. "That's probably how and why this whole story started… she is simply lost in the shadows. After all it was her job. You now, subterfuge as a life choice. The KGB and Stasi still have many secrets and people they call sleepers who are still aligned to their old organisations, and they still link up in secret."

Royston switched the laptop off. "There's no other way than to trace her steps by contacting any friends, family and other links. We can't do that on the ship. We'll wait until we get back and then see what can be done. I reckon we'll have some help via the police... my friend Mike."

"Make sure you phone him direct tomorrow and ask him to get the ball rolling." Michelle moved over to the bathroom. I'll get my office to look at digging into the Stasi file situation. You never know, one of my staff may well have travelled that route."

Suddenly feeling overwhelmingly tired, Royston plonked himself on the end of the bed and flopped backwards. He rubbed his eyes and decided he needed to recuperate before any more calamities reared their ugly heads. As with the earlier mugging, he chastised himself for not seeing ahead. In his heart he realised he was only half focussing on the Turner case; the other half was now spent on his growing closeness to Michelle. It had definitely knocked his concentration sideways but in a very pleasant way. He had not been involved in a serious relationship for many months, and it was all refreshing and exciting to be hooked up again.

Michelle emerged. "I'm bloody knackered." Those sharp words surprised Royston. "Well so am I. I'll clean my teeth and then go to sleep for the next two days."

She gave him a shove as she passed him on her way to the bed. "You're no fun."

CHAPTER FIFTEEN

Royston woke the next morning with the ship rolling markedly. He staggered to the bathroom and staggered back to bed. Michelle was still curled up asleep. He picked up his phone and saw there was a notification for a Whatsapp message. He only used this software sparingly and only because it was guaranteed to be encrypted. This was from Mike McCarthy who had asked when he was arriving back in Southampton. Royston immediately wondered why he wanted to know. He messaged back that they would be in dock in two days' time around six thirty in the morning and able to disembark two hours later. Mike responded by asking him to make contact immediately he landed, rather than talking over the phone.

Royston wondered why the urgency, but at this moment didn't really care... he was beginning to feel a bit queasy with the increased swaying of the ship.

Michelle rolled over to him. "Wow. The Bay is paying us back for all the calm seas we've had. I love this. You really know you're on a cruise ship, don't you?" She jumped out of bed and headed for the bathroom. "See you in a bit. I'm having a shower."

Royston grunted. He remembered he had some seasick pills in his bag. Falling out of bed as the ship heaved in an unpredictable direction, it took a little while to re-orientate. Picking himself up from the floor, he rummaged in his shoulder bag and grabbed two pills. He swallowed them down, and decided to sit still at the desk to try to adapt to the ship's motion. With great concentration he was able to avoid being sick, and ten minutes later as Michelle emerged from the bathroom, he was beginning to feel a bit more sanguine. "That was a close thing. I nearly lost my stomach."

Michelle looked worried. "Oh, is this movement getting to you?" She dried her hair with a flourish. "I love it. A simple breakfast would help you, I think."

Royston shuddered. "I'm not tempting fate… oh no."

"Well, I'm going down to the Lido. I'm starving." Ten minutes later, Michelle gave him a swift kiss on the cheek and disappeared to enjoy her breakfast.

Staying as still as he could, he gradually started to feel more at ease. He hadn't thought seasickness could hit you so quickly… he now unfortunately knew it could." As he sat quietly, hands on the desk his mind started to wander through the amazing happenings of his time on the ship. Beginning to realise just how lucky he had been not to be seriously wounded or even killed, he just had a feeling that something about the whole journey had been very strange… almost as if he was part of a play, over the script of which, he had no control.

He, and now his new partner, had been buffeted by forces that seemed to come into focus and then disappear like wraiths into the shadows. Feeling he had a grasp on some aspects, he extracted his flow chart from his bag, and followed it through point by point, adding the new data about the East German Stasi connections. Sitting back, he was convinced that he had missed something along the way. Reviewing the pathway and notes on his chart, yet again, a hint of a new connection came into his head. Probably nothing, but worth a thought… Jeffery Turner's marriage where his friend, Frederick Bedford was listed as his best man. Could it be that Frederick Bedford was connected to Jonathan Bedford, the MI6 contact he had met in London.

He immediately dismissed this as too far-fetched… but…

Changing tack, he thought through how the two thugs had traced him and attacked him on the ship. As his trip had been arranged at the last minute, his enemies must have already been observing him, to have picked that up. This would imply two things, one, that as soon as he had become involved with Jeffery Turner, they must already have been able to listen in, and two, the heavies had been on board and talking to the communications officer as soon as they had set sail.

All this indicated to Royston that his whole operation was leaky and unfit for purpose. That, he decided, needed to stop immediately. No more open communications, no more chats about the problems and a proper vetting of everyone he had, and would, speak to.

Feeling happier that he was at last understanding the clear danger in this case, he completed his notes and the flow-chart and made himself a coffee. "That shouldn't cause my stomach too much trouble… I hope."

There was one discussion that needed to be had on board before they disembarked. To speak with the communications officer about how he had met the thugs and what he was talking to them about when he had seen them in the Lido restaurant. That still puzzled him and he had not really had answers when they had spoken. He marked this up for further action.

Michelle was back from her breakfast. "Lovely food. Especially made-up omelette, fruit, and maple syrup pancakes. Just the job to start the day."

Royston's stomach churned. "Oh. Don't speak about food. My digestion has just about dealt with a black coffee."

She tousled his hair. "You really don't like this movement, then?"

"Absolutely not. I just need to keep as still as possible and not eat anything." At that moment the ship shuddered as it encountered another large wave, lurching down and sideways. Royston grabbed the sides of his chair, instinctively trying to stabilise himself.

"The talk is that the storm will be over in an hour, so hopefully you'll get through it safely." She stroked his neck. "I don't like to see you looking so pale…"

Royston made his way unsteadily over to one of the comfortable arm chairs and sat down carefully. "That's a bit better. My backside was beginning to go numb sitting in that hard chair."

Michelle laughed. "Is that an invitation to give you some therapeutic massage on that sensitive region?"

"I don't think so, nice offer that that is. I still need to sit pretty static."

Michelle sat opposite him and then got back up. "Do you want another coffee?"

Royston shook his head. "I've gone through my records and flow-chart of all that has happened, and I can deduce that I've been very lazy and a disgrace to my profession by not putting proper security in place, ever since Turner arrived in my office. Even after things started to go pear shaped, I still didn't twig how serious this all was. Just bloody laziness on my part…and I am so sorry I have put you in danger's way as a result."

From what you have said Royston, I don't think anybody could have expected all this from what you say was initially a missing wife investigation."

"I suppose not, but I really haven't been focussing." He smiled. "It's your fault actually… distracting me with your beauty, wit and charm."

Michelle laughed. "I don't know if that is a complement or an accusation? Either way I'm so glad we met and I don't blame you at all. You couldn't have anticipated either attack. Let's enjoy the rest of the trip and then sort this out when we get home."

Royston nodded. "Well, that's all we can do. Hopefully I'll be back in gear when the storm blows over. I am going to spend the next hour or so looking for details on everybody on my list… I'm not going to assume anybody is clean in all of this."

She frowned. "I hope you don't think I was anything to do with it, Royston." She fidgeted uncomfortably at the thought he might have felt that she was in the baddies' frame.

"Of course not, Michelle. I'm talking about everyone who seems in anyway connected with the actual case, from Jeffery Turner right through to the thugs who attacked us… and the communications officer on board here. Everyone that's on my list, even including those I spoke to at home, that is of course everyone except Lucy."

"That's a relief. I would hate to be investigated by you... well not criminally anyway." Smiling, she made her way over to the small table on which the coffee making materials and the kettle sat. Taking a mug, she emptied a coffee sachet into it, flicking the kettle switch on when finished. A few minutes later the water was boiling and she half filled the mug, emptying a sachet of milk to finish. Taking the mug back to her seat, she sat cradling the mug in her hands, shifting her grip as the heat built in the ceramic. "I've thought about this too and it really doesn't seem to add up... mainly because you have not discovered anything and found anyone connected with the missing woman at all. Except of course her Stasi past... but surely the secret services would know all about that and have dealt with any issues on the QT." She shook her head. "It's daft."

The storm was clearly abating and the violent movements of the ship had almost completely been assuaged by the vessel's stabilizers. Accordingly, Royston's stomach seemed to be becoming a connected part of him again, much to his relief. "Michelle, I'm going to have one last conversation with Mark Procter after I've hopefully been able to have some lunch. I have unasked questions of him, and he needs to answer them before we leave the ship."

"Can I suggest that we just chill out until the ship is stable, then we can go to lunch early. You can quiz the guy after that." She sipped at her coffee. "I actually fancy going for a champagne afternoon tea later. Do you want to come? It has to be booked."

"Let's see what I feel like after a slim lunch. I reckon by four I'll be hungry again, whatever. I'll get on with work emails and messages. By then it should be twelve and we can go for some food. That'll give plenty of time to prepare for tea." He smiled and collected his laptop from by the bed and set it up on the desk. He flipped it open and booted the screen into action, impatiently fiddling with the mouse as it started. "I suppose the Wifi is going to be pants, with this storm."

He was right. The static electricity in the storm air interfered with the communications both on the ship and between the ship and satellite, the service he had most expensively connected too on the cruise. After much swearing and frowning, he eventually completed his emails and started on the messages. Mercifully these were few in number and easily answered. Once completed, he stretched backwards and rubbed his sore eyes. "Done"

Michelle had crashed out on the bed and was in fact sound asleep.

"So much for coffee waking you up," he mused. Gently waking her he suggested refreshment of the solid kind. She eased back into consciousness and after touching up her makeup, was ready for action.

In the meantime, Royston had phoned through to the purser's desk and booked an appointment with the communications officer for one o'clock, which would allow time for a light lunch. That agreed he took Michelle's arm and they made their way down the stairs to the Lido restaurant.

Royston collected just a few things he really like, and Michelle chose all the foods he couldn't even think about eating. For the first time that day, Royston felt hungry and ate well. The seas had stopped rebelling and the two of them seemed to be in a happier place. Lunch finished, they made for the purser's office. Michelle was happy to sit and enjoy the music being played by the house violin trio in the lobby while Royston had his meeting.

Mark beckoned him into the inner sanctum of his office and pulled a chair over for Royston, sitting himself behind his small wooden desk.

Royston was ready armed. "Mark, I want to know what you were talking about to the two thugs who attacked me…" He paused, waiting for a response.

Mark shifted in his seat. "When was that?"

"You should remember… in the Lido restaurant in the first few days of the cruise. You were sitting huddled with them and talking." Again, he paused to create a space for Mark to fill.

"Oh, yes. I remember. They caught me when I was doing an officer's walk-around through the decks. They asked me to run through the ships available communications packages… to explain what was the best. I thought at the time that they seemed too knowledgeable for normal passengers who in all honesty don't know one end of a Wifi router from the other."

Royston had to smile as he knew exactly what he meant. His mum and dad seemed to think the Wifi box was magic. "Did they give you any clues as to where they came from or who had sent them?" He knew this was a daft question, but he hoped it might just elicit some useful information.

"No. The only thing we have found out about them, is that somehow they have managed to pass all the security checks, have valid passports and bank accounts, but none of it was genuine. They must have had very top-end support… of course we had no knowledge of that until after their attack on you."

Royston was starting to believe that nothing was going to be gained from the conversation, that he didn't already know.

"One thing, Mr. Fox, one of them had a German accent although his English was nigh on perfect. The other had a Northern English accent… I don't know if that helps."

"It may well do Mark, as there seems to be a German connection." Royston cursed himself silently. He had not wanted to give anything away, and now he had. He could see there was a reaction in Mark's eyes. "Or Scandinavian." He tried to gain the initiative back. "The police think they are a couple of chancers who prey on passengers. Just ordinary old thieves and thugs. That's how it seems to me."

Mark seemed to relax. "We're leaving it to the Spanish and English police, and they have promised to keep us all in the loop."

Royston stood. "Well thanks for your time, Mark." He wanted to terminate the meeting in case he made further boobs. "I'll wait to hear from the police at my end... and thanks for all your help."

They shook hands and parted.

Royston really was irritated by his mistake, even if Mark knew nothing of the Stasi German connection. If he was on the wrong side, he would inevitably pass it on, and his foes would be aware of how far he had progressed with his investigation. He sighed and shook his head as he made way over to where Michelle was seated.

She opened her eyes as he approached. "How did it go?"

"I'm afraid I made a muck up. I let it out that we knew of the German connection. But... he did say that one of the thugs had a German accent but spoke excellent English... which I suspect is usually the mark of a professional."

He puffed his cheeks and exhaled loudly, reflecting his own annoyance.

"It doesn't matter, Royston." She stood and grabbed his arm, tugging him close. "At least it's one all. You know something new, and so does he."

CHAPTER SIXTEEN

Their last two days passed with no incidents. The ship's captain made a visit and assured them that they would be welcome on any future cruise and hoped that the bad experiences would not put them off sailing the high seas again. Royston had actually enjoyed the peaceful parts of the trip, mainly the bits involving Michelle, but the mugging had left its mark.

Royston had parked her car in the same area as Michelle. They both tugged their luggage the short distance to where their cars still sat. Embracing, they were both more than sad to part.

Royston held her close. "I don't want this just to be a holiday romance, Michelle…"

"Me neither, Royston." They fell silent for a moment.

Royston spoke regretfully. "Well, let's get home, sort out where we both are and speak tomorrow. I know I'll have a ton of paperwork to do this week and I'm sure you'll be the same."

She hugged him tight. "I'm going to miss you…I miss you already." Nuzzling her head into his chest she gave a gentle shake of the head. "I hadn't expected this, Royston. I'd thought that after what I have just been through, I wouldn't fall for anyone ever again… and look at me now…" Her voice tailed off.

He held her tight. "Same here."

They stood for a few more minutes and then reluctantly parted, going each to their own car.

Royston had to admit he now felt wretched, not wanting to part with the person who had taken such a grip on his heart. He slung his bags into the boot of his car. Sighing heavily, he sat ready to go. At first try the car started immediately. Slowly driving from the terminal to readjust to English roads he headed back to London. His heart was in his boots and he found it hard to stop thinking about Michelle. Royston shook his head as if to rattle himself into waking up from a dream. He travelled the rest of his journey with increasing familiarity, rapidly re-acclimatising to being back home and all that this would entail.

As he drove, he dictated his thoughts about the cruise into his phone… the Turner case, his own feelings about being attacked and the connections he had made along the way. He carefully avoided mentioning Michelle, so as not to divert his thoughts from the merely practical record of his trip, but also in order not to involve her in his work, as far as possible.

It took three hours to make the journey home after the usual snarl-up on the M25 and then through south London to SW16. The area looked drab after what he had been used to on the cruise. He suddenly felt his heart sink… a real sense of longing and depression started to set in as he squeezed his car into a barely long enough space as near to his house as he could find.

Bundling his luggage through the front door he took a deep breath and gathered up the pile of mail on the floor. He had employed a house sitter for the last week… generally the place looked clean and all in order.

Sitting down at the kitchen table he sifted through the envelopes and advertising. Ninety percent he stripped any plastic wrapping off and chucked into the recycling bin. The other ten percent was bills and personal mail. One letter stood out… his address carefully inscribed in the centre of the large padded envelope. His paranoia surfaced and he felt the package carefully all over. There seemed nothing suspicious, but nevertheless he opened the side with a sharp knife, avoiding any obvious places of entry. Gingerly he looked through the hole he had made into the envelope. It was just papers. Feeling relieved he opened it fully and withdrew the wad of hand-written paper.

There was no evidence of a sender's name or where it all might have come from. On closer examination, he realised that it was written in German, a language which he was not remotely competent in. Frowning he flicked through the papers, noting that there appeared to be a page per named person, none of whom he recognised. He stopped. "I'll get it all translated on line," he mused to himself.

None of the other mail needed his attention, so he prepared a strong coffee for himself and sat in the kitchen sorting out in his mind what needed to be done before venturing into the office. It took two hours to sort out his laundry, hang up his suits and empty the large case he had taken on board. One load shoved into the washing machine and the rest lying in a pile on the floor, he returned to the kitchen table. He grabbed his laptop which was still in his shoulder bag, and plugged it into the mains. Booting it up he thought through how he should get the papers translated. He realised that he needed to scan and perform optical character recognition of the script. He had a professional software version already installed that he thought could deal with the handwriting and translation at the same time.

His scanner-printer was in his downstairs office. He took the sheaf of papers through and after carefully straightening them, fed them as a wadge into the automatic paper feed of the machine. Luckily, there was writing only on one side of each page.

Returning to the kitchen he started the scan software and waited for the pages to slowly feed through the scanner. He had to abort twice when a page skidded sideways and blocked the feed, but third time lucky all twenty-one sheets passed through to be scanned. At the end he saved the file as a picture so that he could then run the OCR on it. He tried his own software but found that because the German was written somewhat stylistically, as it sometimes was in old German documents, the resulting English was unreadable. A few sentences emerged but they could not give him any sense of what was written.

Royston sat back and stretched his shoulders. He became aware that the washing machine had stopped. He emptied it into the tumble dryer and shoved the rest of his dirty clothes into the washing machine and started it up. The combined noise of the two machines forced him to retreat into his office with his computer.

Making himself comfortable, he thought how best to find out what was written on the papers. The obvious answer was to logon to a professional translator, but at this stage he rather felt that keeping it to himself would be the best strategy. He asked the internet if there was an Artificial Intelligence system for reading and translating German. To his surprise, one company was offering such a service as a free Beta trial. If you wanted it done you had to give them detailed feedback on the results. Royston felt that this would be anonymous enough for him to take the risk.

He uploaded the scanned file onto their system and waited as the circular logo spun round and round. He could see that this was not going to be quick. Fifty minutes later he was waiting patiently with his eyes closed and with his arms behind his neck supporting the weight of his head.

"BING". He woke from his reveries with a start. Looking at the screen he could see that a translation had been completed, and an offer to download the result was being offered. He clicked on the flashing button and waited for the file to end up on his hard disk.

He first of all saved the file in one of his companies' encrypted cloud folders, and then secured it with a password. He then opened and started to read it. He was transfixed and sat there reading what he could see were first hand accounts of the Stasi and their henchmen and women, what they did to ordinary people and how they enmeshed family members in their web of deception and violence. Royston knew most of the outlines of what had happened but, this was something several stages more detailed and horrifying.

Halfway through the document he stopped, not believing what was in front of him. Here was an account of how a Fraulein Todt had infiltrated a family known to be anti-communist and had had the whole lot carted off to Russia never to be seen again. There were several pages of horrifying acts perpetrated by this woman... deportations, deaths, imprisonments and oppression of largely innocent people. Royston started to realise that Jeffery Turner's supposed wife was one of the worst that the Stasis had enlisted… and she seemed to be proud of it and wallowed in her successful promotion through the ranks.

He reached the last page. It simply stated that Fraulein Todt had vanished. No-one knew where she was or what had happened to her. The final sentence read "presumed defected." Nothing else.

Royston tapped the desk with his fingers trying to decide what these papers meant and why he should have been the recipient. Clearly someone was following his every move or maybe more than just someone. Sitting abruptly, he made a decision. "I'm going on the offensive… I need to get ahead of the game…" He folded the papers and slipped them back in the envelope. Unlocking the safe, he slid the envelope to the back of the other papers.

He now thought that there must be at least two groups involved. One against him and trying to stop him investigating and another feeding him information which would appear to be helping him to understand what was going on and who were the important players.

Grabbing a piece of scrap paper, he wrote down those for and those against… and indeed those involved but seemingly neutral. This made odd reading as the two who sat in the middle were Mike McCarthy and Jonathan Bedford. All they had done was to grease the path while Royston fell in head first. He was beginning to feel a little uneasy about Bedford, particularly adding in the tenuous but actual name connection with Turner and his 'wife'. It seemed to him that not only was Turner probably not married properly to Todt, but a connection to the secret services did not seem out of the realms of possibility.

He felt it was possible that MI6 had 'turned' Todt and brought her to the UK under a new name and 'married her off' to Turner who was an agent already, for protection. But what could Todt have had that was so important to the secret services. As a member of the Stasi her deeds were obviously recorded in the German Archives and thus open to those with highly accredited eyes, like Bedford. Royston had been given that information in the anonymous papers, but to be honest bad as they were, her crimes were hardly worse than hundreds of others. "Could this be a diversion from what is really happening?" he thought. It certainly felt that way.

Royston realised he hadn't touched base with Mike McCarthy as requested, but decided not to mention the envelope of papers.

"Hi Mike. Just got home. I'm bloody knackered but thought I'd sign in with you as asked, in case you had an update."

"Good to hear you're safe Royston. Sounds as if you were pretty lucky not be dumped overboard." He laughed. "Sorry. I know it must have been horrendous, but at least you're in one piece."

"It was pretty scary, Mike. Have you got anything new for me?"

Mike cleared his throat. "Well it appears that with Turner dead and his wife nowhere to be seen, your role in all this would seem to be finished."

Royston was taken aback. "I don't think so, Mike. They nearly killed me after Turner's death, so there is obviously still something they think I know that they don't want me to divulge… although I can't think of what the hell that might be."

"Yeah. Sorry Royston. You're right, they seem still to be on your case. We'll continue discreet protection now you're back." He paused. "Oh and by the way Jonathan Bedford wants to speak to you… he said it was urgent. I don't know what it is he wants, but I should get over to see him asap if I were you. Fix it up and let me know so I can come along too."

"OK Mike. I'll let you know."

"Nice to have you back Royston. Speak later." With that he rang off.

Royston searched for the card that Jonathan Bedford had given him with his telephone number on. He dialled.

"Jonathan Bedford's office. How can I help you."

"It's Royston Fox. Jonathan wanted to see me as soon as possible." Royston could hear keyboard keys being rapidly struck.

"How about tomorrow morning at 10."

Yes, that's fine. I'll be there." In all, Royston really didn't want to go into the viper's nest, but saw no alternative. This time though he would be better prepared.

CHAPTER SEVENTEEN.

Royston phoned Lucy in the office to tell her he would be back in action the next day. He needed to sort everything out before travelling into town.

"It's great to hear from you, Royston. It seems ages since you left… and so much seems to have happened."

Well certainly a lot has. You're lucky I'm back in one piece actually… well maybe you're not so lucky." He laughed. "Anyway, Lucy, can you sort all the physical mail out into urgent and non-urgent, and I'll deal with the most pressing letters first thing."

"Already done, boss."

"Oh great. Is there anything I need to know now." Royston hoped not. His brain had been half focused on Michelle. He could hear his assistant leafing through some papers.

Lucy came back on line. "Well… there maybe something that needs dealing with, but I think it can all wait until tomorrow."

"Ok, Lucy. I've got to go across to see Jonathan Bedford at ten in the morning, so I'll come into the office first go to Africa house after that… OK?"

"That's fine, Royston. I'll have the coffee ready." She hung up.

Royston sat back in his chair and dialled Michelle. "How are you ?"

"The same as I was a few hours ago, Royston... missing you ." They both fell silent for a moment. "Everything's OK here, except I have a hole in my heart."

Royston was struggling not to go to see her immediately. "Michelle I'd be there in a second, but I must have everything ready for seeing the MI6 guy, Bedford at ten in the morning... I don't want to be unprepared... I need a good night's sleep and to get up all bright and bushy tailed to make sure I screw the most out of the meeting. We'll go out to dinner tomorrow evening and that'll give us both a chance to recover from the trip... if that's OK?"

The disappointment was clear in her voice. "OK... but Royston promise we'll see each other tomorrow evening." Before he could respond, she carried on. "Shall I come over to you in Streatham... or do you want to come here ?"

"Better food where you are Michelle, so I'll come across to you when I'm finished in the office, probably around six-ish... if that's OK?"

"That'd be great. Don't forget your toothbrush !" She rang off.

Royston slept the sleep of the dead and woke at seven the next morning, feeling more lively than he had for a week. Gathering his papers for work he stuffed them in his case and gathered the few extra things he would need for an overnight stay. He had to admit that Michelle's enticements were highly superior to the call of Jonathan Bedford or the office.

The journey from Streatham was worse than he remembered, stuffed carriages, people eating smelly pies and speaking excessively loudly on their mobiles. He closed his eyes and took several focusing deep breaths. "calm… calm… calm…" He tried to isolate himself from the hassle. Eventually they arrived at Blackfriars where he took a blessedly quiet taxi the remainder of the way to his office.

As he entered the door, Lucy rushed up to him and hugged him. "Oh, I've been so worried about you. I thought you might have been killed or seriously injured… " She gave him an extra squeeze and straightened herself up. "Sorry about that. I was just terrified for you."

"Thanks for caring, Lucy." He walked through to his office. "I was pretty scared too… you know when things happen unexpectedly or out of your control, you'd be surprised how quickly bravado turns to fear." He sat at his desk.

Lucy brought him a mug of coffee and placed it in front of him. " I've put the mail in two piles." She pointed to the paperwork on his left. "That lot's rubbish or of not much interest…" She pointed the pile on the right. "You'll be more interested in those." Leaving him to it, she went back to her own desk. "Enjoy."

The 'not very interesting' pile was six inches high and the 'interesting' pile twice that. Royston groaned internally. He shook his head as he started to sort it all out. By the hour's end his desk was clear and his bin full. "Lucy, would you mind bringing me a coffee. I've finished the mail and there's only a few bits for you to pick up." He pushed the small pile of papers across the desk to her as she came and collected his empty mug. "There's two insurance claim forms, four court papers and a potential new client… nothing too complicated." He stood and stretched. Looking at his watch, he realised he would have to hurry his coffee and then scoot over to Holborn to meet Jonathan Bedford.

He had to admit he wasn't really looking forward to the meeting. Finding the man rather supercilious at their first meeting, Royston was determined to hold his own this time round. Bedford maybe held the key to all the ramifications that had emerged since his first meeting with Jeffery Turner.

Lucy returned with the requested drink as Royston gathered papers and thoughts. He had decided not to show Bedford the Stasi papers, as that might entangle him further in the world of the cold war and its consequences. To mention the connection though, he felt would be good ammunition to show that he was at least up with the game, unlike last time. Also, Mike McCarthy wasn't going to be there to hold his hand… he needed to absolutely on the ball this time.

"I can't finish this Lucy, Sorry." He handed the coffee mug over to her and grabbed his jacket and shoulder bag. "I'll see you in a couple of hours. See what you can do with the papers I gave you and then see how our advertising on the website is going… please?"

Emerging from the building into the busy street, he made for the Holborn underground station on the corner of Kingsway. There were crowds of people milling around the station entrance, caused he thought he could see by one of the entrances being closed for some roadworks just outside.

He pushed his way through the melee towards the entrance to Africa House and entered the quiet of the lobby. After announcing himself at the reception desk, he waited a few minutes and was then escorted by Mark the escort or more accurately described, bouncer, whom he met on his last visit. They arrived at the office he remembered from before. Jonathan Bedford greeted Royston warmly. He pulled up a chair for him and they sat opposite each other with the large teak desk in between.

"Royston, I can't tell you how mortified I was to hear of the problems you had on the cruise. We completely missed the ball on that. We underestimated the opposition, what they knew, what lengths they were prepared to go to, to shut you down after finding out what you had discovered. It was unforgiveable on our part and I can assure you that heads are rolling."

Royston was taken aback. He thought that the meeting would be like the earlier one when he alone was in the firing line.

"Our team looking after the operation had not done their homework and simply missed the two thugs that attacked you. Even now we are unsure of who they were working for and indeed why you were so important in the scheme of things."

"Well I was pretty shocked to be attacked twice. The Spanish team seemed slow to react at all times, and how the hell the thugs were able to follow me to Mount Teide without being picked out, really shows a pretty sloppy operation."

Jonathan bowed his head slightly. "Really, Royston, please believe me this won't happen again."

Royston raised his eyebrows as if to say that he bloody well hoped not.

Bedford smiled. "Onwards and upwards, eh?" He pressed a button on his desk. Moments later his personal assistant strode in looking remarkably like Mark the bouncer. "Mark can you set up the projector to show the presentation I finished yesterday, please?" He stood. "Er, Royston we'll sit over here." He indicated two comfortable arm chairs on the other side of the room, both facing a large screen fitted on the wall. "You'll be interested to see this."

Mark set up the short throw L.E.D. projector and slotted in a memory stick. Using the remote control,

Jonathan started his presentation. The first slide headed history of Lotte Elisabet Todt and showed details of the woman's early life in Leipzig right through to her arriving in England and 'marrying' Jeffery Turner. The slide filled in a few gaps for Royston but in all was nothing new. He did note that there was no mention of the other Bedford who had attended the wedding of the two.

The next slide was new to him. It detailed all the people Todt had framed, ratted on and had eliminated, exiled or beaten. The list was extensive and portrayed a vile woman with no morals or scruples, someone straight out of Orwellian dystopia.

From there on the slides gave a broad picture of true intrigue, revenge, blackmail, double agency and up until now a scenario that Royston would not have thought existed in this day and age.

"So how has it been possible to lose this awful woman, Jonathan? Surely she must have been under strict control and supervision?"

Jonathan cleared his throat. "Well that's the rub, Royston… she was under very strict supervision and control… and yet she has vanished. That is not a word I use lightly I can assure you. She has gone completely off radar. We are now assuming that there is another player in the field who has whisked her off into oblivion… but clearly they have felt it necessary to warn us off… and indeed you… in a most risky and careless way."

"Yes, I felt the brunt of that… twice."

Jonathan nodded. "Indeed… indeed. We have tried to trace where your two attackers came from, but aside from them being one German and one Northern English, we have found no trace of them… no identities from DNA, fingerprint or face recognition data at all. They seem to have materialised out of the ether."

Royston shuddered at the thought of his two assailants. "But surely they must have been traced when they left the ship after mugging me ?"

"Again they vanished. We can only assume that there is a hefty organisation behind them... certainly I would suspect that, simply because of the importance of Todt at the centre of all this. Anyway, to the crux of all this in relation to your role…"

Royston wasn't sure that he had or wanted a role.

Jonathan again cleared his throat. Royston recognised this as the man's preamble to bringing up bad news. "Well Royston you are heavily involved and we now want to ask you carry on searching… with full backup from us of course."

Royston frowned. "A lot of use that'll be, he mused to himself."

"We are preparing a much tighter surveillance team to help you, but this will not be obvious to you. They will be there but in the deep shadows, ready to act at a second's notice."

"That's reassuring." Royston was aware that he had inflected sarcasm into his comment. Jonathan gave him a sharp look.

"Look Royston, we are aware of our past mistakes and will make amends, but they are still on your case and if you want to duck out… of course you can. But doing that will relieve you of any protection and I am sure that wouldn't help you to sleep at night."

Royston nodded. "So what do you want me to do, precisely?"

"Just to keep digging as you are, making notes looking in every nook and cranny for this bloody woman. We will follow your every move and hopefully we'll get close enough to her to push her into a trap. He stood and made his way back to his desk. "If you get any contact or clues come straight back to me. Mark will give you a security tag, phone and emergency transponder so that you will never be out of range."

Royston didn't like the thought of that, but at least it might prevent him from being attacked again or saved if he was.

Jonathan put his hand forward. "Thank you so much for helping us. It may be more important than you know. Mark will show you out."

Royston took the hint and gathered his coat and bag. In the outer room, Mark gave him a small pack of electronics, explaining in detail how each was to be used. Royston was impressed with the amazing range of communications they represented and just how small they were. He tucked the box into his bag and left.

Making his way northward towards the underground he had to pause, his way blocked by a pile of commuters all bustling to descend into the underground system.

Royston heard a noise close behind. Turning, he saw a hooded figure pushing through the mele and heading straight for him. His instinct signalled danger. Looking ahead he saw a gap in the crowd entering the tube. He barged through and ran down the stairs, pulling out his travelcard en route. As he arrived at the barriers he thrust the card into the reader and waited impatiently the few seconds before the barrier let him through.

He dared a glance behind.

"Oy. Mate. Let's see your ticket." The ticket inspector standing next to the wide exit barrier put his hand up to stop the hooded figure pursuing him. The follower rummaged in a bag to find the required authentication, and thrust it at the inspector who had taken umbrage and slowed his responses down markedly.

Royston took the opportunity to head down the escalator as fast as he could towards the train platforms. He paused at the bottom... unsure about which way to go, he looked frantically around, settling on the Piccadilly line, a route through to Green Park a stop on his normal route home. He walked fast onto the crowded platform, aiming to stop at the far end near an arch he could use as an escape route if necessary.

Almost immediately a train rolled in. Brakes squealing, it stopped. Royston looked around discreetly and saw the bobbing hooded head moving onto the platform some way back. He pushed uncaringly into the carriage. The wait seemed interminable for the train to pull away. Looking back he could see hoody pushing into two carriages back just in time before the door closed.

This gave Royston a fraction of time to think. The train drew into the next station and the situation hadn't changed, his adversary still where he'd started but clearly alert to any action Royston might take. They reached Green Park with no change when Royston, who knew the area well waited as late as possible and then pushed out the door, onto the platform and headed up the escalator at top speed and into the atrium. Quickly taking stock he headed the for north exit and out onto Piccadilly. He ran up the road to the RAF club, entered and arrived puffing at the reception desk.

He apologised, and told the concierge he was meeting Group Captain Gargett, in truth a long term friend, and asked if he could wait for him. "That'll be fine Sir. The Group Captain is not here yet, but you can wait here in Reception if you wish.

"Thanks." After a minute he asked if he could use the cloakroom.". As quickly as possible, trying not to show his panic, he made his way rapidly along the corridor to the rest room not sure if his follower had seen him enter the building. He was able to see the main door, from his new vantage point with the door very slightly ajar. Two people also wanting to use the facilities gave him strange looks, but he stood his ground and waited until he was pretty sure he was safe.

Returning to reception, he enquired if his friend had turned up. The concierge replied in the negative.

Royston look concerned. "I'll give him a ring.". Moving round the corner and out of sight, he pretended to call Jack. Returning to the desk, he explained that his friend couldn't make it, thanked the concierge and made for the side exit and headed up towards Park Lane, making sure he'd not been followed. Feeling safer now, he walked up to Hyde Park Corner Tube station and set out to go back to his office, but being very careful that he was not being followed.

Arriving Back at Holborn, he made his way up the escalator and out into the open air feeling more sanguine than when he'd set out and sure that he'd shaken off the follower.

Suddenly he felt a painful scrape on his back. He turned sharply. "Shit, what the hell are you doing ?" He saw the back of what he thought was a woman dressed in a dark hoody moving rapidly away from him, pushing her way roughly through the throng. His back suddenly went into spasm and he collapsed on the ground, spilling the contents of his shoulder bag around him. His last conscious thoughts were of someone screaming as he hit the ground.

CHAPTER EIGHTEEN

Lucy made her way to St Thomas's hospital as fast as she could. She had been told that Royston was in the private wing Intensive Care Unit and that she needed to get there fast, as his condition did not look good.

Her heart was racing when she arrived at the ward desk. Immediately she was quizzed on who she was and why she was there.

"You contacted me, actually. My boss, Royston Fox… is in here and is seriously ill." Her eyes filled with tears.

The security guard flicked through the lists on his clip board. "Name, again please?"

"Lucy Strike."

"Yes, we have you down as emergency contact. Have got photo ID? " He ticked his list, checked his watch and scribbled down the time. "The situation is this Ms Strike, Mr Fox has suffered a major allergic reaction to a small injury inflicted on his back. So far we are still running tests, but Mr. Fox is on a respirator and seriously ill. We have not yet identified the allergen but I think we will soon. In the meantime, all you can do is wait."

She wiped a tear from her eye. "Is there anything I can do?" Trying to steady herself, she took a deep breath.

"Nothing. We did find his phone and saw that he had a close friend he'd been seeing, apparently on a cruise from which he'd just returned…"

"That'll be Michelle Baxter… he met her on the cruise and they became very close. Do you want me to contact her?"

He looked at his list. "Err… let me see. Yes, Michelle Baxter…" He made another tick on his list. "Please let her know as soon as possible… it really is urgent."

The quiet of the room was suddenly oppressive. "Can I see him?"

The guard looked over to a colleague sat outside one of the rooms along the corridor and signalled to him. "Go along to my friend over there and he will let you look through the glass, but be prepared …"

Lucy walked rapidly down the corridor and stood outside the room under the watchful eye of a seated guard. He asked her name and phone number and scribbled on his clip-board. Standing, he pressed a button outside the door. The blind lifted on the inside of the window which stretched across the front of the room. Her heart nearly stopped. Putting her hand over her mouth in shock, she could see Royston lying there his skin a shade of light grey. He didn't move. There were tubes and wires attached to him and monitors flashing and pinging every few seconds. The rhythmic clicking of the respirator could be heard over the silence. She turned away and nodded to the guard. "I must get Michelle here… and fast," she said to herself. Walking back down the corridor Lucy realised that she didn't have Michelle's phone number.

Returning to the guard, she asked him if he had details.

After searching her list the nurse dictated the phone number. "I think this was taken off Mr Fox's phone by the police. If not I am sure they can provide it for you."

Lucy couldn't leave the hospital fast enough and outside on the street she took a deep breath and instructed herself to be Royston's right hand in his awful situation. The mere thought of Royston conjured up the vision of him lying there helpless and nearly lifeless in hospital. Tears welled up in her eyes. Wiping them away, she took several deep breaths and dialled Michelle's number.

Michelle answered quickly. "Hello, Royston…"

Lucy butted in. "This is Lucy, Royston's secretary. I'm phoning to let you know that Royston's in hospital… St Thomas's. He's had a massive allergic reaction to something and is in the private ICU there. I can give you the details if you would like…"

There was a stunned silence at the other end of the line. Lucy could hear Michelle's breathing speed up. "Sorry, what has happened, Lucy?"

Clearly Michelle had not absorbed the news. Lucy repeated her comment.

"Oh my god… How did that happen? What was he allergic to ? How is he…?"

"Whoa, Michelle." She made a stepping back sign with her hand as if Michelle was in front of her. "I don't know any more than I've told you. I have visited him in hospital, I' there now. He looks terrible and no-one there is giving anything away, but he is alive and is receiving total minute by minute care. That's all I know."

"I'm coming over straight away, Lucy. Where are you?"

Lucy looked around. "I'm outside of St Thomas's main entrance. I'll head to the cafeteria in the main lobby and wait for you there if you want? I'm wearing a purple coat and my hair is blonde… I'll look out for you."

Sounds of Michelle gathering her things together came down the phone. "I'll be there as soon as possible. The tube will take about thirty minutes… or maybe I'll take a cab. I'm leaving now."

Lucy could hear the stress in Michelle's voice. "Take it steady Michelle and I'll see you in a while." The cafeteria was round to the side of the large lobby area of the hospital.

She queued with impatience and finally was served a steaming hot cup of coffee by a bright and chatty helper. "You all right, love? You look a bit shaky.

Lucy tried to relax. "I'm fine. I've just got a friend come in here and I've been up to see him."

"He'll be alright, love. Don't you worry."

Lucy weaved her way through the throng of tables and chairs and sat down in a place that was visible from the entrance, so that she could see when Michelle arrived.

Cupping the mug of coffee in her hands, she lent her elbows on the table. It wobbled and she had to steady it with her foot. She ran through what she needed to do in Royston's absence. Realising that this might be the continuance of the aggression shown to her boss after the Jeffery Turner meeting, she decided to contact Mike McCarthy. His number was listed on her phone and she clicked the dial icon.

Several seconds later Mike answered. "McCarthy here."

"This is Lucy Strike, Royston Fox's personal assistant. I thought I'd better let you know that Royston is in hospital with some strange allergic reaction…"

"I know, Lucy, but thanks for phoning. We've been protecting him from when he arrived back from the cruise."

Lucy was surprised but relieved that the police were on the case. "Do you know what happened?"

Mike took a deep breath. "Well… despite us watching out for him, it would appear that a person unknown managed to scratch his back with some instrument that had a poison on it. We are unsure what that was or how dangerous it is to his health, but from all appearance it was very very fast toxin… it must have been to have felled him in such very short time."

Lucy was stunned. "Did you catch on the cctv cameras?"

"Yes. It was just as he was entering the tube station. It was a woman we believe but we couldn't see her face. She was obviously a professional as she seems to have vanished from the screens a few seconds later. I'm sure we will be able to pick her up elsewhere, but all that takes time and we want to get her before she leaves the locale. All that's on-going now." He paused. "I've told you too much already, so please do not tell this to anyone else, except perhaps for his new girl-friend. Have you contacted her… Michelle Baxter, I think?"

Lucy was still trying to absorb the details. "Err… yes I've just spoken to her. She's coming over to see him at St Thomas's…"

"Oh Christ. I'll get some backup over to you asap. These bastards are as likely to have a go at you and Michelle, as Royston. It seems they want to eliminate everyone connected…"

"Connected with what?" Lucy had only been on the outside of the Turner case and didn't know many of the details that had unfolded on the cruise.

Mike realised he had already said too much. "Sorry Lucy. I can't tell you any more at present. Where is Michelle coming from and where is she meeting you?"

Lucy was becoming increasingly worried. "She's on her way from Docklands on the underground or taxi and she's coming here to St Thomas's. We're going to meet in the lobby cafeteria. What do want me to do?"

"Nothing. Just stay put for the moment and let us set protection up. We'll speak later but if anything happens let me know on this number… any time, night or day." He hung up.

Lucy sat stunned, her silent phone still in her hand. Immediately she started looking around for suspicious activity. Moving to a place in a corner with good vision of all parts of the room and entrance she sat, exhaled deeply and hid her face behind the coffee mug she again grasped tightly and with her elbows resting on yet another wobbly table.

Some anxious minutes later, she saw a security guard pop his head around the entrance, look around, fix his eyes on her a give a slight nod and smile. She realised that this was the promised protection from who knew what. Feeling a little safer, she checked her phone for messages. Mike had sent a text. "Help is with you now!"

Lucy was on her second coffee when Michelle arrived and came straight over to her. "Are you Lucy?"

"Yes, and you must be Michelle. Great to meet you." They shook hands.

"Royston has told me how good you are as his PA, Lucy. Has he told you about me?" Michelle asked defensively. She sat down breathing heavily.

"A little." Actually Lucy knew next to nothing about Michelle, but it didn't seem relevant now as they were just two women desperately concerned about their man. "Do you want to go up to the ward?"

"Yes, but let me get my breath back." A few minutes passed and then she stood up. "OK. Let's go."

Lucy could see that their security detachment was discreetly following them at a distance. "You might notice Michelle, that we're being followed. It is some security set up by Royston's friend Mike McCarthy of the Met police to protect us."

"What, you mean we are in danger here?"

Lucy pressed the lift button. "Apparently here, there and everywhere. He didn't elucidate further but it seems it's all related to a case Royston was investigating."

Michelle allowed Lucy into the lift ahead of her. "Oh, you mean Jeffery Turner and his wife?"

"So you know about it."

The lift jolted into action, especially slow and grinding designed to carry patients, bed and all when necessary. "Yes, Mike asked me to help doing some online searching. IT security is my business and I must say the on-board system left a lot to be desired. A hell of a lot !! We didn't find much out... but obviously enough for the bad guys to pick up on what we were investigating. Royston also thought they were on his case before he even left Southampton."

They arrived at the ICU entrance and signed in with the desk. "There has been no change, but at least he hasn't got worse." The nurse finished signing them in and directed them back to the room that Lucy had seen earlier.

Lucy took Michelle's arm. "He is asleep and being well fussed over. Don't be shocked at his appearance." Regretting that comment as soon as she'd said it, Lucy back-tracked quickly." He's been sedated to reduce any further spread of the allergen, apparently... until they have the answer to what it was and what they need to do to counteract it."

As before, the guard raised the blind. "Michelle's eyes filled with tears..."Oh my god. What have they done?" She held Lucy's arm tight. "I hope he'll be alright." She took a tissue from her pocket and carefully dabbed her eyes, not wanting to smudge her eye liner that she'd hastily applied before leaving her flat. Realising just how irrelevant that was, she stopped. "This is horrendous, Lucy. Do they know how it happened?"

Lucy reassuringly placed her hand over Michelle's. "Well, Mike McCarthy implied it was some kind of rapid nerve agent given to him by a sharp weapon dug into his back. It was very fast acting, ruling out the more horrible slow poisons… but still horrible."

"Who did it?" Michelle had regained some composure. "They have all those cctv cameras around.. they must have caught the culprit on one of those."

"Yes, they did, but couldn't keep her in sight. They're checking everything right now. It appears it was a woman… apparently a professional… she kept her face covered and out of sight. Mike is going to keep us in the loop as the investigation proceeds but in the meantime doesn't want to take any risks. He is providing close security in case they come for us, but he did say to be vigilant and not go too far from our home bases."

Michelle frowned. "Did he say how and when they'll be protecting us? This is a blanking nightmare Lucy. I'm going to be looking over my shoulder the whole time now."

"Agreed, and no he didn't say what was intending, but said they'd be around at all times." They stayed for a few minutes and the by mutual consent and for protection, decided to leave together. "Shall we go for a brandy Michelle?"

CHAPTER NINETEEN.

Walking arm in arm, they made their way out of the hospital and headed north towards the South Bank. There were watering holes along the way and they decided on a small Italian restaurant which was exuding copious amounts of garlic aroma. They were seated towards the back of the room, at a quiet table with few others nearby.

Michelle looked around at those diners she considered were close enough for scrutiny. "God, I'm getting more and more paranoid by the minute. She took her coat off but kept it on the back of the chair. Lucy did the same.

They sat. The waiter arrived and proffered a menu. He hovered while they made their choice. Ordering a bottle of white wine by mutual consent they decided to eat, but asked for a few minutes to choose.

Lucy breathed out heavily. "At least we can relax a bit here… I hope. We have a security tail, but he's staying outside apparently. He's going to freeze out there."

Michelle looked outside. "Is that him over on the other side of the road looking in shop windows?"

"Yup. I'm sure he's used to doing this." She returned her attention to the menu. Carbonara for me, I think."

Lucy nodded in agreement. The wine arrived and they ordered their food. "So how did you two meet? … I know it was on board.."

"Actually he nearly knocked me off my feet… literally. The ship was swaying about and he was leaving the restaurant. It lurched at the wrong time and he nearly fell into my dinner. Very apologetic and all that, but he immediately came across as a decent human being. Things went from there."

"That all sounds like a holiday romance to me." Lucy immediately realised that she had said the wrong thing. Trying to back-track fast, she stumbled on. "…er I didn't mean that it was all just a bit of fun…"

"It's OK, Lucy. No offence taken. It took us both by surprise in all honesty, me having just got away from an aggressive bully of a husband and certainly not looking for a relationship any time soon. We just got on so well… we just matched perfectly." Her eyes filled with tears. "… and now it might be finished."

Lucy held her hand across the table. "Well, Royston is a fighter and won't give up if given even a slight chance." She could feel herself welling up too..

Luckily the food arrived and after a deft flick of the handkerchief to staunch the flow of tears, they settled down to enjoy the much needed sustenance.

"I'm not sure where we go from here, Lucy. I pretty well know everything about this Turner guy and his horrible so-called wife, but as to who is doing all the aggressive stuff, the focus of that and where it is coming from. I haven't a clue and I don't think Royston had either. There does seem to be an East German angle, but that is far from certain… it may just be a red herring to put us off the scent. I just don't know." She frowned.

"I know he went to see a British security guy called Jonathan Bedford just before he was attacked." Lucy shuffled in her chair as a flash of Royston lying helpless in hospital came into her head. "Bedford works for MI5 apparently, but I am never sure who is who or who works for whom in this crazy case. All I know is that so far, three people have died, one woman is missing… probably the cause of it all, and we are now in danger… and all that because we have tried to find the lost wife… or so it would seem."

They finished off their food in relative silence, both trying to understand how they had ended up in such a precarious situation and in real danger.

The bill called for, they stood to put their coats on.

Looping her scarf round her neck, Michelle buttoned up her coat against the cold spring air. "Lucy. Can I come into the office tomorrow morning. I would feel safer there and with you as well and danger would be halved. I can continue the line of enquiry Royston was on and it might even be a help to you."

That'd be a great idea, Michelle. I'd be really happy if you came in. Do you know where the office is?"

"Yes Royston gave me a business card… all a bit formal, at the beginning. I'm going to travel everywhere by taxi as a precaution and suggest you do too."

They left the restaurant and each hailed a cab. "See you tomorrow morning, Lucy". As she was driven off, Michelle turned to see her security guard reassuringly jumping into his car and pulling out to follow.

Michelle only slept fitfully, even after plying herself with a large brandy before turning in. Nightmares came and went as did her startled response to the slightest noise from outside her apartment. Eventually the night was over and she somewhat wearily dragged herself out of bed. Her mind immediately turned to Royston. She dialled the hospital and after being passed through several layers of interrogation, ended up talking to the desk nurse in the ward. "How is Mr Fox?"

The nurse paused to check the overnight notes. "He's still critical although there has been a very slight improvement in his vital signs… but nothing significant. We are hoping to have the detailed analysis back in a few minutes which might give us the ability to negate the poison precisely. We'll let you know if there is any change."

"So, nothing," Michelle said to herself as she hung up.

She set off for Royston's office arriving a half hour later. Lucy welcomed her and said that she might as well use the main office where a desk had been set up opposite to her own. She nodded across the room. "That's the boss's office." She opened the door and let Michelle in.

"If you don't mind Lucy, I'd like to give the whole office area a scan for transmitters and surveillance equipment. From what Royston said his information processing is leaky… he thought he must have been bugged from the off. I think this is the most vulnerable place for that to happen."

Lucy raised her eyebrows, surprised. "Do you really think so? We are very careful to check all the security cameras each week."

"You have obviously done the right things but modern surveillance is light years ahead of those basics." She started to follow the network cabling back through to the patch box. "For example by simply linking in to your mains wiring, your physical network is an open book to anyone who sets that up." She arrived at the box fixed to one of the outer walls. "This is totally vulnerable simply by tapping in anywhere in the network trunking. Your phone lines will also run through this for internal distribution." She peered inside the box and all around the back and outside. "It doesn't look as if anything physical has been attempted. Let's see about the electronics."

Lucy was now beginning to wonder if Royston had any idea about security.

OK, I'm going to disconnect your desktop from the network while I install some analysis software. It needs to be put on the PC when there is no web connection so that when the machine is reconnected, it can monitor for any intrusions." She unplugged the appropriate cable from the computer, plugged the power supply into a surge protector and filter, to stop hacking via that route.

Lucy reconnected the mains. Michelle then booted the desktop up. Pulling a memory stick from her pocket she proceeded to install the needed programmes onto the hard disc. Once she was sure the software was working after setting up all the details for a VPN and the network monitoring system, she rebooted the pc, before reconnecting to the network.

Lucy watched on. She was good with computers but this was a stage up the ladder of understanding. "Wow. That looks quite an upgrade to our normal level of security."

Michelle waited for the system to fully boot up. Immediately despite the VPN being operational, an intrusion warning came on screen. "I won't actually do anything about that yet. I want to give it a couple of hours for any bad guys to try breaking in. It looks as if you have at least one attacker already though, but I suspect within the hour we'll have plenty more. The trick is to let them in and trace, trap and block them before they realise that you are protected. That deters most of the casual or bot attackers. Then you can concentrate on the persistent ones."

Lucy raised her eyebrows, not fully understanding. "Would you like a coffee or tea Michelle?"

"That'd be great. Coffee please. This is thirsty work." Michelle pulled out a small electronic box from her bag. "I'm going to give the room the once over with a signal detector, just in case you're being bugged in the old fashioned way." She was fast and efficient, not missing even the remotest nook from her search. She arrived at Royston's desk. The detector whined. "Uh-oh." Michelle held up her finger to her lips, picked up a pen and wrote on a slip of paper, handing it to Lucy. "It read ' turn the main office power off and let me know when that's done.'

Lucy obliged and signalled to Michelle.

"Royston's pc is bugged." She took the webcam off the top of the screen. "It's in here. Simple really. It taps into the computer's camera and pc connection. It then not only has power and sound but also video to be hacked. This is a duplicate of the original and this one has transmission electronics which can throw the signal about fifty metres in any direction. There will probably be a receiver box somewhere hidden outside, so that information can be collected without the collector being noticed. It can be tapped remotely from inside a nearby car via a Bluetooth signal. Basic but very effective if not discovered."

She yanked the USB cable from the computer and tucked the offending hardware into a signal proof bag, and placed it in her bag. I should be able to get my boys to find out where it comes from." She turned to Lucy. "Can you reboot your pc again. We'll have to re-start the hack detectors."

Michelle pulled up a chair opposite Lucy at her desk. "As far as I can remember the main protagonist in all of this is the woman who was supposed to be Turner's wife, Lotte Todt the East German Stasi agent, so I reckon we look for hacking traces in that direction."

"I think Royston has done a lot of work on that and I think he had some snail mail related to it in the post when he got back. I haven't seen it though., although he did say it was stuff bout Elizabet Todt and the Stasi." Lucy sipped at her coffee. "When you think we're secure, I'll log onto the company cloud backup and see if there is anything there. He always stored files he wanted to keep under wraps and really private, there."

"Chances are, Lucy, that the bad guys will already have found anything saved there."

"Oh god. Is it that bad?

Michelle nodded. "Yup. That bad." She sipped her coffee and sat thinking things through. She looked at her watch. We'll give it another hour and then see what we've got."

Lucy nodded. "I'm starving. Shall I order some noodles in from across the way."

"I think it'd be better if you go and get them personally. Less likelihood of being poisoned, that way." She laughed, but realised that it was a bit more than a joke.

Lucy took a credit card out of the petty cash box and put her coat on. "What do you want? I usually get a veggie Pad Thai."

"That'll be fine, maybe with a couple of flat breads or plain dumplings."

Lucy left the office. Michelle leant back and closed her eyes. She was tired to her soul and was only keeping going through sheer doggedness and the hope that she could help Royston. Dozing off, she was woken by Lucy's return. She shook her head to wake herself up. "Oh sorry, Lucy, I just dozed off. I'm completely knackered."

Lucy unwrapped the food and emptied it onto the plates, handing one to Michelle. She also handed her a small bag. "There's your dumplings. They look nice, but I'm trying to cut down on carbs."

They chatted distractedly as they ate. Clearing up the remains, Lucy sat back down at her desk. "The software says it has traced four hackers and twenty seven bots. What are bots?"

"Oh yes, sorry. Bots are artificial intelligence software hackers that autonomously trawl through the internet in search of unprotected data on important computers and networks." Michelle went round the desk to look at the screen. "May I sit down?"

Lucy gave up her chair. "Yes of course. I wouldn't know where to start."

"Hmm. These all look like amateur hacks and the bots are all standard. Nothing too nasty there. We can leave the system on overnight and see what we get tomorrow…"

The phone rang. Michelle answered the call. "Who is it , please?"

"St Thomas's here. May I speak to Lucy Strike, please?"

CHAPTER TWENTY.

Lucy grabbed the phone. "Yes? Lucy Strike here."

"We would like you to come into the hospital, there have been some changes in Mr Fox's situation and we think you may be able to help with the next stage."

Lucy was shaking. "What sort of changes?"

"We'll tell you when you get here. We think it is important that you come as soon as possible."

"I'll be there as soon as I can get there."

"Thankyou. Come straight up to the emergency medical ward ICU."

Lucy fumbled with the phone, struggling to replace the instrument she was shaking so much. Standing for a moment with her eyes closed, she used her yoga experience to calm her. "Oh god. I hope he's alright."

Michelle handed Lucy her coat. "Well they didn't say he was dead… that has to be a good start." She chastised herself for the lack of subtlety in her remark. "I mean… that's really good news and will probably mean he is through the worst."

Lucy buttoned up her coat. "Can you come with me, Michelle. It'd make it all a bit easier… keep me on the straight and narrow and hopefully stop me dissolving into tears."

"Well if that's what you want, I'd be happy to come. We're partners in crime on this."

The journey was tense, both women fearing the worst. Arriving at the hospital they made their way to the emergency medical ward and then the ICU. To their surprise, they were met by Jonathan Bedford with two security guards attached.

"Ah, hello." He surveyed the two women. "I'm Jonathan Bedford. I work for the Government and know about everything that's been happening." He stepped forward offering his hand. "You must be Lucy, Royston's personal assistant..." He Turned to Michelle, "...and you must be Michelle, Royston's new partner. Very nice to meet you."

Michelle immediately went on the defensive remembring that Royston had put a question mark over Bedford's head with his possible connection to Jeffery Turner and Elizabet Todt's best man at the wedding. "What's the news?" she asked calmly.

Jonathan guided them over to some chairs in reception away from the main desk. "Well, Royston has been taken off life support and the amount of sedatives knocked back." He looked up for a response from the two women. They both stayed calm. "It is looking as if the prompt action of the paramedics saved his life and their rapid actions were so effective that it appears he may make a complete recovery... despite the powerful poison that was used on him."

"Wow, that's fantastic." Lucy couldn't contain herself. "That's brilliant."

Michelle remained silent waiting for any bad news which she felt must be coming.

Jonathan continued. "But, and it's a big but, we don't know if he will suffer from some form of amnesia. It often follows such a poisoning... we'll , have to wait and see." He paused again. "If you want to we can go in an see him. He's not awake but your voices may well get through and hasten his recovery."

Michelle could feel her heart racing at the thought of seeing her man. "That'd be great, Jonathan." She tried to keep a calm exterior.

Jonathan strode over to the desk and spoke to the duty nurse who turned and pointed to the room, the glass window of which they had looked through at Royston the day before. As they approached, the security guard stood and waited. Jonathan nodded at him and the door was opened.

The room was quiet. No more clicking and whirring, the sound of the artificial breathing unit that was an embedded memory from the last visit. Royston lay there peacefully but horribly inert, no flicker of consciousness.

Michelle approached. "Can I hold his hand?". That question was rhetorical as she was going to hold it anyway. Royston's skin felt only slightly warm to the touch. Michelle squeezed it between her two hands, tears welling up as she felt no response. Speaking quietly to him, inaudible to anyone else, she urged him to come back to her in one piece. She kissed him on the forehead and backed off.

Lucy tentatively moved to his side, a mixture of emotions flooding her thoughts. She gave up any pretence of being distant and prudent. Hugging his hand , she quietly pleaded with him to wake up and come back to them. Her eyes shed tears and she tried to wipe them away, only achieving smears of eye shadow. Trying again she turned away so as not to let the mess she had made of her face be seen before she could remedy the situation. "How fragile we are," she said to herself

Jonathan had stayed discreetly quiet as the women spoke to their man.

"OK. I've a bit more information for you. Shall we go outside?" Jonathan opened the door to let them out. They silently trooped from the room and returned to the table they had sat down at earlier. "We've heard from Germany... the Stasi Registry Office... and they have given us a wad of documents they believe form the basis of a serious case for the prosecution of Elizabet Todt. A list of accusers and details of all her activities for the Stasi, and victims claims."

Lucy frowned. "That sounds an awful lot like the papers Royston received in the office on his return," she whispered to Michelle, who immediately stiffened, glancing at Lucy with a slight narrowing of the eyes as a warning to stay silent on this."

Jonathan continued, unaware of the reaction. "We think that all of this maybe down to her enemies wanting her to be caught and punished... but why they are after Royston we don't know. He hasn't anything to do with this on the surface... of course there may be an angle we've missed and he has some unseen involvement."

Lucy was indignant. "Are you suggesting that Royston is involved in some way we don't know... I doubt that, as he's been the one attacked all along. That's ridiculous."

"Yes Lucy, but that's on the surface. What is the underlying connection with Royston. Only he can tell us, and he hasn't done so, so far."

Michelle chipped in. "Well I think that's ridiculous too. Royston has been attacked... indeed so have I, and as far as I can see neither of us are secret agents."

"Those are the operative words Michelle... as far as you can see. These things go on under the radar and only a tiny few know what is really going on. Smoke and mirrors."

"That doesn't make any sense." Lucy butted in. "This all started when Jeffery Turner came into the office and asked us to find his missing wife, who turned out to be this Stasi agent Elizabet Todt... what have we all got to do with that?"

Jonathan stayed silent for a moment. "Hmm. I can see that's what has happened from your perspective, but not mine. Royston has been the focus from day one. Why did Turner come to Royston, and why was he chosen out of all the detectives in the city? Why was he mugged and why nearly killed." He drummed his fingers on the table. "It all points to him being more deeply involved than you know."

Michelle shook her head. "Well I'm going to prove you wrong, Jonathan. I think you are completely mistaken, and I intend to show it."

"And me," Lucy added assertively. "I agree completely with Michelle."

Jonathan stood up, clearly annoyed. "Well only time will tell." He slid the chair under the table. "Stay in touch." He strode out of the ward.

Michelle and Lucy looked at each other. "We can't have him going after Royston. We'd better get on with it before old misery stumps up some false accusations just to prove his point." Lucy actually felt empowered by the meeting. It had given her the motivation to dig deep into the whole affair, with no inhibitions about where it took her.

Michelle felt the same way. "Let's get back to the office and get cracking. We'll sift through everything we've got so far... but to be honest we've pretty well done most of what's been possible."

"One thing that I haven't really looked at, is why the office was disturbed early on when Royston was on the cruise." Lucy frowned. "I told him about it, but he didn't think it was anything other than the cleaners moving stuff out of the way. Now, I think it's worth a bit more thought."

"Actually, Lucy I'm pretty knackered. I need some sleep. Shall we go back to my place and start over early in the morning. I've got plenty of space and a nice spare bedroom. It would be sensible to stick together at the moment... you know, strength in numbers."

"Not a very big number though, Michelle." Lucy laughed, allowing the tension of the day to drop below boiling point. "Let's get a cab back to the office. I always keep a well stocked overnight bag there in case Royston ever wants me to rush off somewhere to get some papers or interview a client. We can go from there to your place if that's OK?""

They hailed a cab and directed him towards Holborn and then on to the beckoning safety of Michelle's flat. As the taxi drove smoothly across the city, Michelle noticed a black Mercedes flollowing. Her mind flashed back to Tenerife and the horrific car chase. "Oh my god. They're after us again." She gripped Lucy's arm in panic.

"Who are, Michelle." Lucy was startled and looked back out of the rear window. After a few seconds, she turned back to Michelle and laughed. "Don't be daft. It's a little old lady driving her limo."

Michelle released Lucy's arm, feeling very foolish. "Sorry. I just thought it was the same lot that followed us in Tenerife."

"Not unless it was the 'granny mafia'." She laughed again, lowering the tension.

"Ha ha. Very funny. Sorry about that." Michelle relaxed back in her seat.

Arriving at the office, Lucy jumped out of the cab and collected her bag. A few minutes later she reappeared carrying a large holdall which she bundled into the cab ahead of her.

"You weren't kidding Lucy, were you. Have you got the kitchen sink in there?" Michelle laughed. "Thanks driver. Can we go on to Lincoln Plaza now, please.

After adjusting herself and her large bag, Lucy peered out onto the crowded streets. "How far to go, Michelle?"

"About five miles. Should be about twenty to thirty minutes from here."

They talked through the possibilities as they zigzagged through the narrowing streets, eventually arriving in the tangled mass of huge buildings that is Docklands. Michelle lived in Lincoln Plaza, just south of Canary Wharf and right in the middle of the huge area now housing many tower blocks and business houses. She had inherited it from her father who had died disastrously young, shortly after divorcing his second wife. It was his final home and now it was hers. The flat was spacious with three bedrooms, an open plan living space and a superb view up towards the main docklands area. At night the view was spectacular.

Finally, the two arrived as close as possible to the Plaza, and after thanking and paying the cab driver, made their way to Michelle's flat.

As the evening was drawing in, the view was quite spectacular as indeed was Michelle's apartment. Ultra-modern, spotless and beautifully furnished. Here's your room Lucy... all on-suite. When you're ready come on through to the lounge. I'll open a bottle and we'll order some food in if you like."

"Sounds like a plan." Lucy disappeared into her room and sorted her bag out, emerging ten minutes later looking refreshed and relaxed. "Great idea to come here Michelle... thanks. I do feel safer."

"The security is second to none here. That's why my dad chose it. He was involved in providing high-tech security on a grand scale for tower blocks, of which this is one."

"Mm. I'm glad about that with all the scary goings on we've had to go through... or at least you and Royston have." Lucy fell silent. "Really... thanks for this. I feel safe here."

Michelle poured out two glasses of Chablis. "I'm sure you'd do the same for me... maybe that'll be needed sooner than we think." They touched glasses. "Here's to sorting the buggers out."

CHAPTER TWENTY ONE.

The following day brought good news in the form of the hospital reporting that Royston was off the critical list and rapidly moving towards full consciousness. His memory was a little impaired, affecting the details of very recent memories, not being able to recall the attack or anything after. The actual process of remembering functioned normally, but random small details were missing.

On wakening, Royston had been told in no uncertain terms to stay in bed despite professing to be one hundred percent. His medical team were still unclear as to whether he would suffer long term effects and insisted he stay put until they were sure, much to Royston's annoyance. Additionally, his case was so unusual and rare that they wanted to gather every possible piece of information on the effects of the Conotoxin, fearing that this attack would not be an isolated incident. They compromised on him staying two more days, although after a single day of full consciousness, he was allowed out of bed to walk around, albeit with the security guard in tow.

He tried to insist on contacting Michelle and Lucy, but security was under strict instructions not to allow any external contact. Jonathan had total control over everything that was now in place. "Royston, you've got to understand that this is our best chance of flushing out Elizabet Todt and anyone who is working with her..."

"That may be so, Jonathan, but I have two important women thinking I'm critical and who knows how worried and stressed they are..."

"Sorry Royston, but you are under my care and supervision. There is going to be no external contact at all until I am ready. We've set up a network of surveillance and protection to flush Todt out, but it's not quite complete, so for now, you are to all intents and purposes, on your death bed."

"That's not the point, Jonathan. I must tell the grls I'm OK..."

Jonathan cut in. "No chance Royston. This may be our only chance to crack this group, and I'm sorry, you are not going to mess that up. I'm sure they'll survive another few days without your loving care."

"Don't be facetious," Royston responded angrily. "It's completely unacceptable..."

"Sorry, it's not going to happen." Jonathan turned to leave the room. "You've now got an entertainment area next door so you don't get bored." Indicating the room to the left of Royston's, he left. "Ciao."

Royston was fuming but had to accept that he had no power to do anything, basicly a prisoner in a hospital with no way out. He sat on his bed, defeated, his emotion battered beyond any experience.

Lucy and Michelle had gone to the office early to see what could be done and to deal with any business. Having heard nothing, they were becoming more and more desperate. Despite Michelle's best efforts, emotion was overcoming her.

Lucy did her best to comfort her friend, but she wasn't much better herself. "We've heard nothing and Jonathan hasn't updated us since yesterday. What the heck is going on." Lucy feared the worst, hoping beyond hope that her boss was alive. "I'm going to phone Mike McCarthy." Unsure if Michelle knew about him, she added, "Er... he's an old friend of Royston and has been involved with this mess from the beginning." Tapping the connection on her mobile, she waited for an answer.

A minute later Mike responded. "Hi Lucy. Mike McCarthy here. What's news?"

"I was phoning to see if *you* knew anything, actually," replied Lucy, surprised.

"No. I've no updates. As far as I know Royston is still in isolation and can have no visitors. What have you heard?"

Lucy frowned. "Zilch. Everything seems to have gone blank and we're really worried… that's why I've phoned. Jonathan Bedford has really warned us off and is refusing to give anything away. He won't even let us know if Royston's on his deathbed or will be out tomorrow… absolutely stubborn and insisting that any news is going to be kept in house."

Lucy could almost hear Mike thinking. "He is a bit devious, that one…

"Devious," Lucy exploded. "He is the most aggravating, stubborn and insolent man I have ever met. He squirms more than a bag of rats. Everything has to have a hidden meaning or connection…. To him, people don't seem to matter."

"That's a bit harsh, Lucy. Trouble is, that's his job. He's a senior MI5 agent and sees things from a totally different perspective to us or anyone else except perhaps the Russian FSB."

"That's not our problem though is it ? Michelle and I need to be kept up to date and Jonathan is the only one holding the reins!"

"He needs to realise that we count, not just his beloved spy setup." Michelle was feeling very frustrated with Jonathan's stone wall attitude.

"Well, sorry I can't help guys. I don't know anything more than you." He paused. "Maybe I'll go round his back… I know a few people that might be happy to help. I'll get back to you asap." He rang off.

Lucy sat at her desk. "That was useful then… not."

Michelle nodded. "The only loose end we have, is the unexplained re-arrangement of the office when Royston was away. Thinking laterally, maybe that was someone trying to find something. You know, Jeffery Turner was in that office for a round half an hour before Royston turned up. If his intention was to leave something here as a safe and secure hiding place, it would seem he made a good decision. Let's make a thorough search through his office… you know looking in all the not-so-obvious nooks and crannies."

They both went through into Royston's office. Lucy looked around for likely hiding places. "I reckon we should do this logically, so that we cover every inch of the room." She pulled out a piece of paper from the printer. "I'll draw a plan and we can list and tick off every inch." Drawing a outline of the room she glanced round to make sure every inch could be recorded."

Michelle peered at Lucy's drawing. "That's all very well, Lucy, but we don't even know what we might be looking for."

Lucy looked up. "We can narrow it down somewhat, as Turner wasn't carrying anything when he came into the office, or at least nothing that wouldn't fit into a coat pocket."

"OK. So if he was hiding information, what would the likely format be if it wasn't a bulky folder of papers or photos." She paused, thinking. "What about a memory stick. That could hold a huge amount of info on one stick."

Lucy nodded. "That sounds about right. So we need to look in all the places that one of those could be hidden. I'll start with the desk and you have a look at the book case over there." She nodded towards the large built in shelving by the window.

They remained silent while focussing on the hunt but after forty five minutes they had come up with nothing.

"Let's have a coffee and think again." Michelle poured two mugs from the pot of fresh coffee out in Lucy's office. Handing a mug to Lucy, she sat on the edge of her desk. "What if we are looking for something too big. A lot of mobile phones have midi or even micro SD cards that can be as big as a memory stick, memory-wise. You could download all your info onto one of those. The smallest are about the size of a little finger nail. That would open up a whole new set of places it could be hidden."

"Hmm. That's a good idea. It could be anywhere without ever being found." She sipped her coffee. "I'll go over the desk again and you look at the bookcase with the potential tiny size of the object, in mind."

They chatted for a while and then returned to the task in hand.

Lucy sat at Royston's desk and thought. She opened the front drawer where he kept bits and pieces and absently pulled out a lump of Bluetack, squeezing it between her fingers as an aid to thought. Suddenly she stopped. "Michelle, I think I've got something here." She pulled out a large plastic box of drawing pins and paperclips. She carefully examined the box, shaking it several times to rearrange its contents.

Emptying them carefully on the desk, she spread it all out. There amongst the pins were two micro-SD cards. "Gotcha." Lucy picked them out dusted them off, holding them for examination.

"Wow. That's brilliant. Let's see what's on them."

Lucy scooped up the pins and paperclips and funnelled them back into the box, returning it to the drawer. "I think I've got an adapter that these will fit into. It came with my camera." She returned to her desk in the outer office and rummaged around in one of the drawers. "Ahh. Here we are." She held up the adapter. Placing one of the micro-cards into the space available, she slotted it into the side of her laptop. Waiting a few seconds, her software checked the card for bugs and then showed a page of complete gobbledegook on screen. Lucy frowned.

Michelle looked on. "The card and files have been encrypted. We'll not be able to unencrypt them here, but I can get my team on to it if you want."
"Agreed. I want to know what all this has been about. To hand them over without finding out, would be against my principles… unless of course we can't unzip them."

Michelle took the two cards and used a disk copy programme to back their contents up, putting the files on the cloud fully secured with double password protection. She then put them in a safe envelope. "If you like, I'll courier them over to my team and see what they can do."

"Will that be safe ? What if they 'watchers' get wind of what we've found?" Lucy was genuinely worried.

Michelle picked up her phone. "I've got codes to tell my team that this is a security imperative." She dialled, spoke to one of her team without saying what she wanted them to do. Ringing off she sealed the envelope in a Jiffy bag and taped it up. "They will pick it up and have a look."

"You told them to do that, all with those few words?"

"Yeah. We have to deal with some very secure items , so our conversation code has all the instructions embedded in key words."

Lucy raised her eyebrows. "I think you should explain that to Royston. He's the least secure person I know."

Fifteen minutes later a courier arrived to collect the package. Michelle handed it over and phoned her office. Again her sentences didn't match the situation.

Lucy looked quizzical. "I asked them to give me the heads up at the first sign of anything recognizable from the memory cards. There's nothing we can do until they let us know. Shall we go for a spot of lunch and a glass?"

Lucy grabbed her coat. "Is the Pope a Catholic? There a great Italian in Great Queen Street. Shall we walk down there."

As Lucy opened the door she was startled by Mike McCarthy standing outside, just about to enter.

"Oh. Sorry to startle you Lucy. Just thought I would pop in and see if you'd heard anything."

"We're just on our way to lunch."

Mike stepped back to let them out. "I can join you for a few minutes. I'm on duty."

Walking down Kingsway amidst the bustle of midday, they chatted, although neither Lucy or Michelle said anything about the memory card. Entering the restaurant, they were escorted to a table at the back of the room and relatively quiet. Sitting down, noisily dragged the wooden chairs across the similar floor, they slung their coats over the back of the chairs. They ordered a light lunch and a bottle of wine.
Mike just had a coffee. "So tell me what's been happening." Michelle and Lucy looked at each other discreetly.

"A big zero, Mike." Lucy shifted in her chair feeling guilty about lying. Trying to divert the conversation towards Royston, she asked Mike if he'd had any joy with Jonathan.

"Not a sausage. They've shut the whole thing down… no-one in and nothing out. We simply don't know how he's doing, but I suspect if he was not getting better and still non-communicating, they'd be more open. They want to keep him out of sight to flush out the bad guys, I suspect. I still have my spies out trying to discover what is going on, but Jonathan runs a very tight ship."

"We've gathered that, Mike." Michelle took a sip of her wine. "We still don't know why they are after Royston though, do we?" Michelle was fishing.

"All I can imagine is that they think he has something of great importance, and they are determined to get it…" Mike glanced at the two women. "You have no idea if there was something given to Royston by Turner… do you? Could be anything…a book… some papers… a hard disc…"

Lucy flushed.

Michelle spoke to divert Mike's attention. "He never said anything about that. Indeed we did discuss the reasons for the mugging on board and came to the conclusion that they were obviously looking for something specific, but Royston didn't have a clue, what. They gave him and his belongings a thorough going over and didn't find what they were looking for… either, why would they still be after him?"

Lucy's ears had ceased to radiate heat. "Yes, he never said a word about Turner having left something for him… and I was there. I saw nothing."

Mike shrugged. "Well, keep looking." He drained his coffee cup and stood and stretched. "OK you two. Let me know if anything comes up and I'll do the same. I'll ring tomorrow morning regardless. See you later."

He left, leaving Lucy mighty relieved. She was no good at lying.

CHAPTER TWENTY TWO.

Royston had had enough. He spoke to his security guard. "Can you get Jonathan or someone with the right authority here, please… now."

The guard, with whom Royston had established a good relationship, realised he was now dealing with an increasingly irritated and angry man. On balance he felt it would be a peace saving move to bring Jonathan into any discussion he was about to have. "Hang on, Royston. I'll call him up." The guard clicked on Jonathan's number on his phone. After a short wait the call was answered.

"Jonathan here. What's the problem?"

"No problem sir. Royston wants to discuss his release, and I thought it best to bring you in."

Bedford clearly didn't want this. "Well tell him he can maybe come back into public life tomorrow after I have completed the security ring…"

Royston was listening and on hearing this took the phone. "Look Jonathan," he retorted furiously." This is ridiculous. I need to get my life back… I have friends and family who are in limbo until they know I'm OK. Just let me go."

Jonathan sounded exasperated. "I have told you I am not releasing you until the coast is clear and we have built a ring of security around you. If they succeed in killing you, we will have learnt nothing and you'll be dead." He sighed heavily. "Just be patient… and tomorrow morning you can go… but we will need to release the info overnight so that the story spreads slowly and in a low key way so that we can flow who reacts and who is likely involved in the aggression."

"OK Jonathan. But that is it. From there I take my chances and look after myself."

"Royston. Do not underestimate your… our enemies. There is a lot more at stake here than meets the eye. We'll aim at eleven hundred hours tomorrow then." With that, Jonathan abruptly terminated the conversation.

Michelle and Lucy finished their lunch and returned to the office. Michelle was about to contact her team when her phone rang. She answered. "Hi boss. We have sent you a secure message over the office link. You'll be very interested."

"Ok." Michelle closed the call. "Lucy. Is it Ok if I use your laptop… the one I 've put the security detector software on ?"

"Of course." Lucy stood and let Michelle sit in front of the computer.

Fidgeting to get comfortable, Michelle started the encrypted communication app and waited for the connection to signify that it was safe to link to the companies saved files. After a minute sifting through the list she saw two folders entitled 'Michelle SD-card-1' and another 'Michelle SD-card-

2'. "Bring a chair over, Lucy. I think they have managed to decrypt some files."

Lucy eagerly took up post at Michelle's shoulder, peering at the screen.

With trepidation, Michelle opened the first folder. A long list of files appeared each titled with a name. She opened one. They were both silent as they read the contents. It was a detailed file about the named person with information about profile, location, relations, work…everything, but most damning a final paragraph in red, labelling the person 'STASI' and FSB asset.

They were both stunned. Opening several other files, they realised that this was a list of agents or potential STASI/FSB agents active in the West. They were old, but the list was huge. It couldn't be ruled out that some may well still exist and be active foreign spies.

"This is way beyond our pay grade, Lucy. No wonder there has been such huge ructions over this." Staring intensively at the screen as the list of files scrolled down, Lucy spotted something. "Hold it, Michelle. Go back… I think I saw the name Todt…"

Michelle found the file and clicked on it open. They were both stunned. There it was in black and white… Elizabet Todt, STASI now FSB agent in the UK… married to Jeffery Turner a British agent. The word 'ACTIVE' stood out.

"Bloody hell Lucy. The bitch. She is a double agent, pretending to be giving the West info on the Russians but actually infiltrating the UK security service as a an FSB asset." She sat back, thinking of the implications of these files and of Todt in particular.

"No wonder they were going mad to get these files back… they're dynamite. I don't think we are safe until this information is in the hands of MI5. This is scary stuff…"

"I'm going to tell my team to make twenty copies of the files, encrypt them separately and send them to key storage centres, so that whatever happens they will be safe from deletion. My team is good. They'll know what to do." Michelle immediately contacted her base and gave them very clear instructions. "That's done. I feel happier that the info cannot be stolen or deleted by anyone. I can have it in the public domain at the click of a button should anything happen. We have contingencies for the preservation of such data."

"I'm happy about that, Michelle." Lucy had to admit she wanted to be a million miles away from such explosive information. She realised what was now at stake. They were both and indeed all three including Royston, in the middle of a spy war of national importance. Jonathan had been right to be very wary indeed.

Michelle was absently scrolling down the list of files. "Hold on. Oh my god. There's a file headed 'Bedford'." She was shaking. "Surely he can't be a double agent... and he's been in on everything from the beginning." She hovered the mouse cursor over the file, undecided if she wanted to know if the erstwhile 'Jonathan Bedford' was a foreign agent. She shook her head. Lucy stayed silent. She opened the file.

'Frederick Bedford' was the name on the first page. Both women breathed out with relief. "So who is that then?"

Lucy jumped in. "He was the Bedford who acted as a marriage witness at the Turner - Todt wedding. Royston picked it up early on but nothing ever came of that line of enquiry. Thank god it wasn't Jonathan Bedford. The world would have collapsed if he is a double agent."
"Look here." Michelle pointed down the bottom of the file. "He had a 'trade name' of Resting American... I wonder if all of these agents have such names? That does imply some wider international connection to all of this, but I suppose that's only to be expected."

"Do any of these files have photos attached?"

"Not the ones I've seen... but maybe some have got them that we haven't opened."

The door-phone rang.

"I'll shut this down and break the link so there'll be no record of what we've seen." She closed the software down, cleared and overwrote all the temporary files and reverted to the bland front screen of day-to-day work.

Lucy clicked the connection to the door video. The screen filled with Jonathan's face. "OK Jonathan you can come in." She pressed the door release. A few minutes later, Jonathan appeared in the office.

"Hi there Ladies." You would have thought that there had been no animosity between them. "Good news. Royston is being let loose tomorrow and I thought I'd bring the good news myself." He waited for a response.

"That's brilliant." Michelle felt a zing of adrenalin curse through her system. "When will that be?"

Jonathan looked pleased at the response. "Tomorrow morning up towards mid-day. We are managing the media and hope that no-one will particularly respond. We are of course monitoring all connections we know of, so I really doubt if anything dangerous will occur as a result.2

Lucy was delighted. "It'll be great to see him. Has he had any lasting adverse reactions to the poisoning?"

"Luckily for him, as I said a few days back, the paramedics saved him from the worst." Jonathan scratched his chin. "The medics will continue to monitor him over the next couple of months just to be sure." He looked over at Lucy's computer. Lucy immediately felt her ears flush red. "Have you come up with anything new?"

Michelle took control. "No. Nothing. We've been waiting to hear from you… if you knew what we should be looking for."

"No. We haven't had any indications of what the baddies want. I suspect it has been lost… whatever it was... when Turner drowned. We'll keep looking anyway and please do the same… and let us know of anything unusual."

Both women nodded, hoping they weren't looking too guilty. "Of course." Lucy crossed her fingers.

Jonathan turned to go. "Well please keep all of this quiet and do not send emails or messages out to people about Royston's return to normal life. Let's keep it as low key as possible." With that, he left.

Lucy let her shoulders relax. "Phew. That was very hard. I nearly gave it away. I'd never make an agent in the field." She sat at her desk. "Could I suggest we trawl through the files… and names, then list any people we think might be involved with the Turner case. After all we have found Todt and Frederick Bedford. Maybe if we are a bit more thorough, we might find someone else playing the double game."

"Good idea Lu. And then we'll go home and have some food. I'm pretty hungry again." She took back the seat at the computer and restarted the secure software system. The list of files came back on screen. After an hour, Michelle rubbed her eyes. "Bugger all. There's probably nothing more than we

210

can find here. We've twenty files to go so let's finish them and go home." She stretched and re-focused.

Lucy concentrated, watching closely as Michelle ran through the remaining files, something made her stop. "Hold it Michelle. Is that file named Hendell? That name has cropped up before…" She thought hard and shook her head. "No, can't place it but let's flag that one up anyway. It has to be there somewhere in the old grey matter."

Tired but much happier with the prospect of Royston's return the next day, they closed everything down and made their way back to Michelle's flat.

"Shall we order in a couple of pizza's Michelle. I just fancy some comfort food."

"Great idea, Lucy. I'll order up when we get home." They fell silent for a few moments as the taxi wove its way through town. "This has been a very strange day indeed. We are at the centre of an international spy scandal … and talking about pizzas." She laughed. "How ridiculous is that?"

"Well, as long as we stop being targets, that would help. I just need some time feeling safe and secure… I need Royston back at the reins. I'm not being a wimpy woman, but he is at the heart of the problem and has a better viewpoint on how to navigate through these things… I'm just his practical help."

Michelle nodded. "Yeah. Royston's presence would be an asset… even if he was only someone to blame

!" She laughed, allowing some release of tension. "It's going to be great, but I'm not going to put any pressure on him to sort all this out. That is in Jonathan's hands and he needs to step up to the plate."

"I absolutely agree. I think that for a so-called professional he has been more useless than a chocolate fire guard… bloody hopeless actually. So, yes. He needs to bust his backside."

Arriving at the flat, they locked the door behind them and secured it.

"This is a great flat, Michelle. I'm quite jealous although I love my cosy space. This is something special."

Michelle tossed the keys into the basket by the front door. "I'm really lucky with this…" She indicated the whole flat. "… from my dad and a load of money from my bastard ex. I can do what I want and not feel the pinch. Not that I want to stop work though, I'd go stir crazy." She took a bottle of Sancerre from the fridge. "Do you fancy a glass, Lu?"

"Defo." Lucy sat on the sofa. "I've been thinking. What about considering working with us at the agency. I know you are involved with your company, but I get the impression that it can work well on its own. We need someone new to add to the team… you know, to add new thinking and direction."

"Mmm." Michelle poured two glasses of wine and handed one to Lucy. "There's a thought. I quite like that idea, but I'll need to feel secure in my relationship with Royston… you know with me effectively on the bounce." She fell silent for a few moments. "Hell Lucy, that sounds a really interesting idea. I'll think on it and when the time's right we'll all speak about how that might work."

CHAPTER TWENTY THREE.

Royston was ready to go at five a.m.

His security team thought otherwise. "Royston, Jonathan has said eleven this morning so that's when it'll be."

"Well I can't see how a couple of hours will make a difference." He was not in a good mood and was desperate to escape the secure hospital ward he had be locked down in, since he'd been attacked. The longer his captivity lasted, the more frustrated and irritated he became, despite chastising himself for his lack of control.

He sat at his laptop and in a desultory manner flicked through the news on screen. Suddenly a picture of him came up under the heading, 'Unusual poisoning victim recovers fully.' The story read like a fantasy about how he'd been stung by a cone snail at a tropical fish sellers after picking one up thinking it was an ordinary sea snail. Royston snorted. "What bollocks," he said to himself. "Non-one is going to believe that !"

He moved on to other news and eventually closed the screen down and sat back. He could hear the familiar voice of Jonathan Bedford entering the room behind him.

"Ah. Royston. The time has come to release you into the wild, again. Have you got everything bagged up?"

"What you mean my toothbrush, razor and laptop?"

Jonathan gave a weak smile. "Well whatever you have here, anyway. We're going to take you to your office with no fuss and no publicity. According to everyone's knowledge of what has happened, you have been poisoned by a rogue cone snail at a tropical fish supplier. That covers all bases, I think."

"A bit of a thin story, to my mind, Jonathan. People aren't mugs."

"Yes they are. If they believe the rubbish that appears on many news screens, they'll believe this." He sat down opposite Royston. "Anyway we don't really care what the public think, we are more concerned with our enemies. It is absolutely vital you now focus on trying to find whatever it was that Jeffery Turner left for you to find, wherever it was and whatever it was. That is the centre of this whole business and it is down to you to sort it out."

Royston frowned. "You mean it is down to the man who has no resources and has been mugged, chased and poisoned and imprisoned, to do your job ?" He looked at Jonathan. "I don't think so."

Jonathan held up his hands. "Well what do you think I can do sitting in my office?"

Royston realised that he was on to a loser. "Well, as long as you protect me and the girls, and provide us with some tangible support, I'll do my best. Can you do that?"

"Of course Royston. I have promised that already, but it is you who now needs to get ahead of the game and come up trumps."

Royston gave an ironic smile. "You're a master of platitudes, Jonathan. All I can do is make as much progress as I can and report anything I find, to you."

Jonathan stood, picking up his case. "I am sure you will. I'll be in contact anyway, to give you a progress report, daily. My team will now sort you out and get you on your way, and…," he proffered his hand, "…and thanks again Royston."

Within an hour, Royston was speeding in a taxi towards his office, accompanied by yet another security agent. This one seemed much more proactive than the previous, checking every step of the way and not allowing Royston to poke his nose out, before the way ahead had be carefully surveyed.

The cab drew up outside the office and Royston was swiftly manoeuvred inside the building and into a fully checked office. As he entered, he saw Michelle and Lucy standing to one side. They had been instructed not to move until the all clear was given.

"A bit of overkill here," whispered Lucy. "Also about a month too late."

"OK, Royston. Clear to go. We'll be outside the office and discreetly in the locale, in case of any action from the bad guys." The guard left and the room fell silent.

Michelle rushed over to Royston, hugging him tightly. "I never thought I'd see you again." She tightened her arms and closed her eyes, just enjoying the moment.

Royston held her head close to his chest. "God." He took a deep breath. "This has to end." He could feel her tears of joy soaking into his shirt. "Fabulous to be here."

Lucy came over and hugged them both. "These have been the worst days of my life, Royston. We really thought we'd lost you and when that b…., when Jonathan stopped giving us information, we could only suppose the worst."

"Well, I'm going to finish this once and for all… whatever the cost. I can't spend the rest of life looking over my shoulder."

Lucy wiped tears from her eyes with the back of her hand and sat down at her desk. "Well we have some information that even Jonathan doesn't. We found what Jeffery Turner left in the office."

Michelle allowed Royston to step back and sit on the edge of Lucy's desk. "Yes. We reckoned that he must have left something and it was this that the heavies were looking for. Since nothing had been found even after quite a bit of searching, we went back to the beginning." She nodded at Royston's office. "Turner was in your office for half an hour before you met him… plenty of time to hide something away in a difficult to find place."

Lucy took over. "We thought carefully what would be the easiest way to store masses of information in the smallest format… and no, not the old-fashioned micro-dot of James Bond fame." She smiled. " So… we thought that a micro SD card would be the best. That changed the way we approached the search and after some scrabbling about looking for such a thing, we actually found two tiny cards mixed in with your pot of paper clips and drawing pins. You would never have found them in any search other than a really detailed one, and only then if that's what you were looking for." She paused.

Royston was all ears. "Go on."

"Well. We passed them on securely to Michelle's team who were able to used their sophisticated algorithms to decrypt the contents. So far they have only told us about the first, which appeared to be a long list of FSB agents, many ex-STASI personnel, who are now agents in the West."

"Bloody hell, Lucy. Do you mean that we have a list of enemy agents in the UK…?"

"And all over the West," interjected Michelle. "We don't know what the second card had on it yet. We haven't heard from Michelle's team."

"Well let's get onto them." Royston looked at Michelle.

"No. We'll wait for them to contact us. They'll do that as soon as they know they've cracked the code and have something to tell us... they don't need prompting."

"OK. Sorry Michelle. I'm eager to get ahead of the game."

"Anyway Royston, we're actually not being very sensible here. We need to be careful as we found a whole load of bugging stuff here… in the office. In fact I think it would be sensible to give you the once over in case someone had bugged you."

Royston smiled. "You're kidding."

Michelle pulled out her portable signal detector. "Stand still, Royston." She carefully ran the scanner over Royston's clothes.

"Be careful where you're putting that thing, Michelle." He laughed.

She continued tracing the scan head slowly over his clothes. They all held their breath. "OK. Nothing. Did you bring that bag with you?"

Royston nodded.

"Bung it over here then."

He fetched the bag and placed it on the table in front of Michelle. Checking the bag in detail, she stopped and frowned. "There's something in there… but it's not reading with any signal I know. Can you take all the items out and lay them on the table, here." She indicated Lucy's desk.

Royston obliged, feeling his stress levels mounting.

Michelle scanned each item with great care. She picked up his toothpaste. "There's some sort of signal coming from that… it doesn't seem to be a transmitter, but it is definitely radiating something."

A shiver ran up Royston's spine. He remembered the Russian agent Litvinenko and the radioactive Polonium 210 poison that had been use on him. It was administered in a cup of tea. Perhaps this was another way they used to get rid of enemies. "I wouldn't go anywhere near that, Michelle. It's possible that the contents are radioactive, which is why it's showing up as non-standard radiation. Is anything else showing up?"

Michelle pushed the offending toothpaste tube over the edge of the table and into an empty waste bin. "I'll put this outside the window and the window sill. That should be far enough away to keep it safe." Returning to the table she carefully checked everything. Nothing else seemed to contaminated in that way.

"We need to call in Jonathan, I think, and quick." Royston hesitated. "Although it was only his team who had access to this bag… I'm going to call on Mike instead." He grabbed his phone….

Michelle knocked the phone out of his hand."

"What are you doing?" Royston asked, looking across at Michelle.

"I've just picked another signal… looks as if it's coming from the direction of your phone. Don't touch it. Scoop it into that bin over there and stick it outside the window. Go and scrub yours hands… now !"

Gingerly, Royston did as he was told. "For god's sake. Are you sure there is nothing else contaminated?"

"Pretty sure, now ." Lucy , used her phone to contact Mike. She outlined what had happened.

Within ten minutes, Mike with a full hazard team turned up at the office. No fuss just a team of experts. They took the offending items and placed them in lead-lined boxes, and ran a Geiger counter over everything in the room including the occupants. The team leader finally spoke up. "You've all had a very lucky escape… all of you. Your prompt action has saved you from a very grisly end. Somehow your goods have been contaminated with Polonium 210… you may have heard of that… a favourite of our FSB friends. Mike has told me about your links with a spy case, so we must assume you are in the firing line."

The offices were minutely examined for any contamination. Luckily only the two items had any risk attached to them and they were sealed and had not leaked any Polonium outside. The team leader indicated that the job was done and there was no residual radiation in the offices. He loosened his hazmat suit. "I need to link in with MI5. Who is your contact there?"

Royston looked at Mike. "I'm not sure. They just contact me when and where they need to speak to me."

Mike raised his eyebrows, questioningly. "I'll take the lead on this. You've got my contact details. Just let my office know what has happened and I'll link in with MI5 myself."

The team leader nodded. "OK, but we need to have direct contact when the full analysis comes through."

Mike had realised why Royston was being cagey about MI5. "Er, no. You'll feed all information, and I mean all information to me directly and you will have no contact with MI5 directly. This is my case and nothing goes anywhere without my say so…" He looked hard at the team leader… "Is that absolutely understood?"

"Yes sir. Everything through you. We'll have the analysis results very quickly and they will be sent through to you only…"

Mike looked him in the eye. "Great. That's fine."

The hazard team left with no fuss, but Mike stayed in the Office. "OK, Royston. What's been going on here ?"

After a lengthy explanation, Mike fully understood Royston's hesitancy. The only possible source of the radioactive material was from the place Royston had been held and protected in, and the only people there were Jonathan's team. "So what you are thinking is that MI5 has been infiltrated by possibly FSB people who know that you are probably the only person who knows how Turner is linked into Elizabet Todt and perhaps her old STASI accomplices."

Royston nodded. It was now or never to tell Mike about the data cards that Lucy and Michelle had found. "Mike can you give me two minutes with Lucy and Michelle, and then I can update you on everything… is that OK?"

Mike nodded.

"We'll go into my office for a moment." Lucy and Michelle followed Royston and closed the door.

"Michelle, I need to be guided by you and your team on this. Have they found anything new on the second card ?"

"I've just had a text saying the files are all named photographs of various people on the other card."

Royston rubbed his forehead. "Bloody hell. That means we have a list of names and pictures of enemy agents in the UK or maybe we are meant to think that.. I am not sure whose given what, to be honest."

Michelle nodded. "I agree. I also know we are out of our depth … this is an international issue and we need someone we can trust on our side. I think it's worth taking a risk with Mike. He hasn't put a step wrong all along the way and has helped when asked. My vote is that we go with him. What do you think Lucy?"

"I agree. I did have some doubts early on, but he has done nothing than be supportive and helpful. Like you, I thought early on he wasn't on our side, but since then he has been dead straight."

Royston looked at both of them. "So it's agreed then. We'll let him into what we've found and all the other details, and ask for his help… Yes?"

CHAPTER TWENTY FOUR.

Michelle and Lucy returned to the main office. Michelle took the lead. "Well Mike. We have found what Jeffery Turner left in the office. It was two micro SD cards… they had detailed descriptions of agents of the FSB who are now here in the West. The list looks to be old but never the less contains the name and details of Elizabet Todt. She has clearly been planted by the FSB and is only pretending a defection. That makes her an enemy agent… big time. There are also other names we seem to have come across such as Frederick Bedford, who also looks like one of theirs."

Mike took a deep breath. "Well that might explain why this has been so important to the bad guys to shut down. They obviously think that Royston is the only one who knows about the information and are dead set on getting him out of the equation."

Lucy joined in. "Yes, Mike… and we now have, or at least we hope we have pictures of them all. The problem is, who do we trust with the information… especially as we think MI5 in the guise of Jonathan Bedford may have been infiltrated. How are we going to find the right person to tell."

"That's my job, Lucy." Mike was feeling as if his role was now pivotal in securing the right response to this new information. He too felt that Jonathan and his colleagues were not to be trusted, even just until they'd been cleared of suspicion. "I know another route to the top of MI5 and I'll now use that… in fact that is our next move. I'll get in touch with my colleague." He picked up his phone and then put it down again. "On second thoughts, I'm going to use our secure line at the Met offices." He stood.

"What shall we do with the information we've already got?" Michelle was uncomfortable at the thought of her team being directly in the firing line on this. "I have told them to make twenty copies of all the relevant data and securely store them all on the cloud and in a number of other places."

"Good move, Michelle. I will need sight of the data as soon as possible but I'll ask my MI5 contact how best to communicate it. I'll get back to you asap." He looked around. "Has Bedford put any security in place for you all ?"

Royston nodded. "Yes, but if he is suspect, and he has allowed this radioactive stuff to pass his system, then I wouldn't have much hope of that being any use."

"I agree, Royston, so take extra precautions and if you can all travel together and go to the same places, that would probably be the best strategy until we can give you the all-clear. There's significant safety in numbers. I'll also detail a couple of my men to shadow you and keep an eye on Bedford's lot. We'll speak in a short while." He left the offices.

Royston sat heavily in one of the chairs. "Well what do we do now?"

"I'll try to arrange for the photos on the second disk to be transmitted through to us securely, so that we will at least have some idea if anyone else we've been in contact with, is a bad guy." He looked over to Michelle. "Can you do that ?"

"Yes. I'll do that now." She sent a text to her team and waited for a response which came back almost immediately. Michelle read the contents. "OK. They've sent a link to the encrypted files on our cloud storage system. We can access those without fear of hacking through our security logon. She looked around. "Shall we have a look?"

"Absolutely." Royston and Lucy moved their chairs over to the desk where Michelle's laptop sat. They spent the next hour looking through mugshots of many rough looking men and women.

Lucy sat back, stretching her shoulders. "I can't see anyone I can recognise."

"Hang on, Michelle. Go back one picture." Royston leaned forward to get a better view. "I recognise that that guy…" He tapped his fingers on the table, trying to recollect when he'd seen the man. He shook his head. "I know I've seen him… but where?"

"You think, Royston, and we'll move on a bit, or we'll never finish." Face after face stared at them with not a spark of recognition. Michelle paused for a moment. "I don't know any of them, but then maybe that's a good thing."

Royston sat up sharply. "I know where he was… he was with Jonathan Bedford when I first met him in his offices in Kingsway. He called himself… er…" He tried to remember. "It was a German name. Bedford said he was from their German office… yes. He was Herr Hendell and he had a woman with him. She was also German. She called herself Frau Schmidt.. that's a dodgy name if ever I heard one."

"So he or even they could be FSB agents inside MI5," Lucy asked.

"Looks like it . I wonder if we can find the woman, Royston." Michelle resumed clicking through the pictures.

Royston rubbed his eyes. They were beginning to feel sand-papered. "Hey stop, Michelle." Again he peered closely at the screen. "That's her…Frau Schmidt. What is the name under the photo? I can't read it from here. Oh my god. It's Todt…"

They all fell silent. This was the missing wife of Jeffery Turner. The STASI, FSB, MI5 double or triple agent. They were face to face with the cause of all the grief they had been through. A hard looking face with no compassion evident in the blank eyes.

"We are in trouble, guys. She was the 'Frau Schmidt' from Bedford's office. That means his whole operation is compromised. I'm glad we chose Mike and not Bedford to bring into our confidence. Can we print off the two photos of the Germans so that we can send them to Mike. He may be able to find out where they are and what they're up to."

"Definitely." Michelle downloaded the pictures and saved the. "I'll Save the pics as secure files and send them over to Mike immediately."

That done they agreed that they must stick together at all costs so as not to allow any of them to be picked of like Royston had been. They were all in this together.

Lucy wet over to the kitchen area and filled the coffee machines reservoir with filtered water. "Do you guys want a coffee?"

"Yes please, Lucy. My brain's fried." Royston stood and stretched. Taking the photos from the printer he took the copies and put them in the safe. "I think we need to hand the whole lot over to Mike's team as soon as possible. The sooner the better to my mind. I'd really like to meet this Todt woman, if only to look her in the eyes to show that I'm still standing."

Michelle took a mug of coffee from beside Lucy. "We'll let's leave that confrontation until they are safely secured, eh?"

Lucy passed a cup to Royston. "Agreed. I don't want to meet them until I know they can't get at us."

The tension in the air subsided. Royston had spoken to Mike and passed on the photos and details of the two Germans whom he recognised as well, from the first meeting with Bedford. Agreeing that they must be very careful until the two had been collared or at least nullified, Mike had promised to be as careful as possible with the handling of the information. Now he had realised the true scale of the problem, the enormity of the implications were overtly apparent.

"I think it would be a good idea to go back to Michelle's flat. It's really secure and we can then decide on what we need to do next."

Lucy agreed. "But what about Royston? Can you fit him in overnight as well, or do you need me to go to my place?"

"There's plenty of room, and as Mike said, we need to stick together… for safety." Michelle finished her coffee and washed the cup up. "I think we should go over there now and think strategy. Our next move is going to be largely in Mike's hands, so we need to be somewhere that we can be safe and think clearly."

"OK. Let's go. I'll call our usual cab company and we can be pretty sure that if I ask for my usual driver, that we'll be safe." Royston picked up his holdall and then put it back down. "I'm not going to take that.. there's probably some other nasty surprise mixed in with my stuff. Maybe Michelle I can order some bits and pieces for delivery at your pad ?"

"Sure. We can get a premium delivery from one of the Supermarkets. You can get everything you need that way. I also have a throwaway phone you can use."

Lucy switched everything off, set the alarm and locked the door after they moved into the hall outside the office. She still felt quite nervous about going anywhere but the three stuck together and found their cab waiting outside. They could not see any security personnel in the vicinity but a third sense told of their presence, unseen.

Their tensions ebbed away as they were transported out to Canary Wharf. Arriving at the flat, Michelle organised the accommodation, giving everyone their own room. It was not the time for romance.

Royston ordered the essentials and sat back on the sofa. "This really is a nice pad, Michelle. Don't fancy a lodger do you." He laughed.
"I don't know you well enough, Royston. Maybe in a couple of years." She roughed his hair up.

"OK. Let's decide on our next move… first of all what are we going to eat. I'm starving. I only had the standard hospital breakfast this morning and nothing since."

Lucy clicked on her phone. "What about a pizza or two with some garlic bread? Simple and filling."

"I'm up for that Lucy. How about you, Michelle?" Royston was already salivating.

"Fine by me, but I don't want chillies in it if that's OK."

Lucy phoned their order through. "It'll be about twenty minutes, is that OK?"

"That's fine. I'll get us some beers." Michelle went through to the kitchen and a few moments later appeared with glasses and bottles. She passed them around and sat down in a an armchair. "Phew. I'm knackered."

"Is it OK if we have the tele on, Michelle. I want to get up to date with the news if that's OK."

"The remotes on the table." She pushed it in Royston's direction. He leant forward and took it, clicking the buttons to bring the large TV into action.

Watching the news was always a bit of a chore these days, thought Lucy, with many of the so-called newscasters wanting to be the news.

After fifteen minutes viewing, Michelle turned to Royston. "Anything you didn't know about?" Michelle smiled. "I don't think you'll be too out of date… same old same old boring rubbish, in my view."

"Yeah. Don't disagree, but I still like to see what has been happening… in this case you're right… nothing." He flicked over to an antiques program. "Let's all get bored with this."

Lucy shrugged. "From my viewpoint, guys, I think we need to firm up what we can and cannot do. I think we are totally dependent on Mike to protect us and particularly you, Royston. Until then, I think we should stay put and only move anywhere after we've told Mike our plan. In that we he be sure of where we are and also be warned that we need protection. So the next move is to wait to see what he comes up with."

"Sounds like a plan." Royston nodded. "I agree. We need to be ultra patient.. no unplanned moves… then he can keep things safe."

The doorbell sounded. Michelle stood. "That'll be the pizzas." She went through into the hall and peered through the door eye, and opened the door.

A gun pointed at her head. "Don't make a sound or you're dead." A slight German accent warned Michelle not to question the command. She stood rooted to the spot. "Tell your friends it's the pizza delivery… and don't make any attempt to warn them."

Michelle's throat was dry and she croaked a message that it was the pizza delivery. The intruder whisked her around and forced the barrel of the gun into her neck. "Now move."

CHAPTER TWENTY FIVE.

Royston froze as he saw Sebastian Hendell pushing Michelle into the room at gun point. He could see her shaking and pale.

"Sit down with the others." Hendell shoved her unceremoniously down onto the sofa.

Elizabet Todt appeared round the door and walked casually into the room. "So you are the bunch that have given us so much trouble. It would have been better for you to given us the information we were looking for. As it is, you're going to end up the same way as Turner." She had cold eyes and a steely voice.

Royston was desperately thinking of a way to signal for help.

Hendell pulled up a dining chair and reversed it, straddling the seat and leaning on the back, the gun dangling casually over the top. Looking from one to another he stayed menacingly silent. "OK. What we want is all the copies of the lists that Turner gave you." He raised his eyebrows. "You do have that information, don't you?" He banged the gun menacingly on the top of the chair. "I really do hope so."

Royston decided to tell him exactly what they'd done. "Well, Hendell, those files are now in the hands of MI5 and the Met police. They have been stored on the cloud in encrypted files with instructions given to our staff to release them if I don't contact them daily to assure them that I'm in one piece."

Hendell laughed, "That's all very schoolboy, Mr Fox. We've followed everything you've done and are really only here to take a bit of revenge for exposing us. So how shall we begin… a shot through the knees, pulling a few finger nails out or crushing a glass into the face of your women." He stood. "Yes I think the latter would teach you a lesson in real espionage." Moving over to the drinks table he grabbed a glass and made a move towards Michelle. Royston made to stop him. "Don't be stupid Fox." Hendell levelled the gun at him. "Do you want to die and still have your pretty lady disfigured?"

"You bastard, Hendell. We've done nothing to you." Royston sat back with the utmost difficulty.

Hendell grabbed Michelle by the neck. "And now pretty one, let's see what shattered glass can do to that beautiful complexion."

Michelle screamed and Royston leapt at Hendell who turned in a flash and fired the gun. Off balance the shot hit Royston's left arm passing right through the biceps and thudding into the sofa leg. Royston was able to continue his lunge, catching Hendell off balance and sending him sprawling across the floor, the gun sliding into a corner.

"Scheisse." The German scrabbled to get up but slid on a mat.

Royston gained his balance first and kicked out at the head of his assailant. His foot landed with a solid thud on the side of Hendell's head who landed unconscious against the coffee table. Too late Royston looked round, only to be hit with a bottle by Todt. He tried to fend off the blow but only partially managed to. His arm was now bleeding profusely and he was feeling very light headed. Todt stood over him ready to deal another blow.

Royston wasn't sure how, but Todt collapsed beside him. He was just aware of Lucy wielding a cast iron frying pan, before he passed out.

Both Michelle and Lucy bound the two Germans with a tow rope that Michelle had stored in the meter cupboard. They made good work of securing their prisoners. When they regained their senses they were attached to the door handle and totally unable to reach the multiplicity of knots securing their hands and feet, and looped around their bodies. Lucy had secured one piece of cord around their necks and looped it over the door to pull their heads up into a heavily strained position.

They were pleased with their work. "We've called Mike, and he'll be here as soon as he can."

Royston tried to clear his head. "What?" Slowly the fog parted and his arm injury started to ache big-time. "I'll need a tourniquet on that. Have you got something we can use."

Michelle disappeared and returned with a big roll of bandage. "I had this when I turned my ankle over.

It's stretchy but should do the job." She wound it tightly round his upper arm above the wound which was oozing blood at a steady rate. As she tightened the bandage, the flow slowed and stopped.

Royston winced as she finished the job by giving the bandage an extra turn. "Shit. That's really painful."

"Got to be done Royston or you'll bleed to death. I think the bullet's nicked an artery."

There was a noise at the front door. Jonathan Bedford appeared in the doorway, made a quick survey of the scene. He produced a gun and grabbed Lucy. "You bastards." He directed his venom at Royston. "You have no idea what you've done." With that, he coshed Lucy on the head and dragged her out of the door where one of his men bundled her down the back stairs.

It all happened so quick, that neither Michelle or Royston had really taken in what had just happened.

"I need to go after him, Michelle."

She held his arm. "No. You're in no fit state to go anywhere. Mike'll be here very soon and can go after the bastard."

Royston had to admit he couldn't do anything even if he caught Bedford. He was utterly drained and fading fast. Michelle guided him to an arm chair. "Now sit still and we'll get Mike's team onto it."

As if on cue, Mike appeared through the door. "What the hell has been going on." He looked around and then saw the two Germans. "Oh. These must be Hendell and Todt. Good work guys."

"Bedford has taken Lucy... I think as a hostage. She'll be safe as long as we deal with this carefully. He'll lose his security if he kills her." The mere thought of that, made Michelle shudder. "Has your team followed them?"

Mike shook his head. "This is the first I've heard of it. How long ago?"

Michelle frowned. "A few moments... no more than five minutes. How come your team missed them ? They must have run right past everyone."

"Not if they went out the back... there's a tradesman's exit and van port. He probably had a van waiting with authentic looking driver. I'll one of my team to take a quick look at the CCTV and get the ID of the van or car... whatever it was." Miike pulled his walky-talky out of his pocket and issued instructions. "We need to get Bedford as he seems to be the king pin in all this, particularly as he had these two in his office right under our noses. No wonder we felt that every move of yours was being second-guessed."

The reply came through a few moments later. "Ah. They've got an ID on the van. It appears they're heading down south, maybe to Gatwick or a smaller airport like Biggin Hill. That is the normal exit route for these types. We'll have every exit point covered before he can get anywhere." Another call came in. "That's some good news. Lucy appears to be OK she's secured but not injured by the look of things."

Royston took a deep breath. "Thank god for that, Mike."

"What do you want us to do?" Michelle was eager to help.

"Nothing you can do except wait. I'm going back into the field so I want you to stay put and not go anywhere. I'll keep you up to date as we move in. But don't answer the door unless it's for me… understood?"

Royston nodded, feeling foolish in the extreme having let the very people they were chasing into the flat. "OK. I get the point."

Mike left and the flat suddenly seemed empty. A few moments later a group of security police arrived to collect Hendell and Todt, who despite much cursing were carted off peacefully enough.

Michelle tidied everything up trying to restore some normality. She sprayed the blood stains with remover and threw the towel away with which she had used to staunch the blood flow after Royston was shot. Picking up the broken glass from Todt's attack, she also dabbed up some of the wine that had come from the bottle. She used a distinctive serviette taken from a pile on the drinks table. It bore a single red logo on one edge and she was careful not to smear that colour on the wine soaked light coloured carpet. The whole clear up took over an hour, during which time no news came through. Royston was increasingly worried for the safety of his P.A.

At last Michelle's phone rang. She clicked on 'answer' and turned the speaker on. "Yes?"

"Mike here. It seems Bedford has escaped in a different direction. We hit the van but it was being driven by an innocent decoy. We're now looking in other directions for him. Sorry to be the bearer of bad news. We'll speak later." He rang off.

"Oh for fuck's sake, Michelle. Can't they get anything right? How the hell did they make that mistake?" Royston's adrenalin was up and he was feeling much more like a fight.

"I don't know." Michelle put her phone on the table. "So if he didn't go in the van, how did he escape unnoticed with security all around the block? He couldn't have used another car with Lucy in the boot and simply disguised himself… could he?"

Michelle sprung up. "I know the security manager here. He'll show me the CCTV footage if I ask nicely. Let's go down and see what we can find out."

Royston heaved himself up and followed Michelle down to the security office. She knocked on the door which was answered by the manager.

"Hello Miss Baxter. How can I help? Are you all OK now after the ruckus?"

"Well we're here still. Mr Fox has been injured and I need to get him to hospital, but first I wanted to see the CCTV footage from about an hour and a half ago. We know Mr. Fox's P.A. was abducted and we want to see if there are any clues on the video."

The manager looked startled. "But I thought it was all OK. We had the police in here looking for the same thing. Did they get it wrong?"

"Yes. They were deliberately misguided and want us to take a second look and see if we can gather anything new." Michelle extended the truth a bit to add to the urgency of the request.

The manager opened the review software on a big screen in front of them. Here's the playback from earlier… about the right time. You can see the van that the police were looking at. A man dressed like Bedford emerged from one of the bay doors and pushed the person he was accompanying into the back of the vehicle, then jumped into the drivers seat and skidded out of view at speed. Then nothing. The other vehicles were still.

"Royston frowned. He must have gone out of here… he must. There's no other way."

As he was saying this three people came into view Two men either side of a woman. One of the men tested the door of a small SUV and opened it. The other directed the woman into the back and got in with her. The other man drove. They were not dressed like Bedford or Lucy had been, so the scene looked innocuous.

Royston exhaled loudly and was about to turn away when he saw the woman drop something discreetly out of the window. Looking closer he could see it was a hanky or serviette. He immediately recognised it as one like that used by Michelle when she was mopping up. "That's her… that's Lucy. He pointed at the screen. What's the registration number and the make?"

The security manager looked closely at the screen and magnified the scene. He had to de-pixelate the screen to be able to read the number plate. "It's SOU 688 I think. Yes that's it. Must be a private plate. And it's a black Mercedes SUV… a GLB I think."

"A black Mercedes. That'd be right," thought Michelle with memories of Tenerife coming back. "We need to let Mike know immediately." She again pulled out her phone and reported the news to Mike.

"OK. Michelle we'll find it. Those have trackers on if the car is stolen. I'm close by you at the moment. Do you want to come with me in case we can pick them. Lucy will need some friendly faces… if she makes it."

Thos words pierced Royston's heart. He couldn't think of life without Lucy. "Yes pick us up." He was feeling passable but still wobbly, but this was more important than anything he'd suffered himself.

A few minutes later, one of Mike's men rang the bell and hurried them down to an un-marked police car. "Mike was driving. Hi guys. God, Royston, you look shit. Are you Ok for a chase?"

"It's Lucy, Mike. What would you do?"

Mike grunted, put up his blue lights and raced towards South London. "We've picked them up heading down on the M23, luckily there's been an accident and the traffic is still static southbound. If we're lucky we can sneak up on them pretending to be attending the crash. They've been spotted jammed in the middle lane and going nowhere. They may even be going to Gatwick, but I don't think so. It's too easy to get trapped in that mess."

Michelle made sure her seatbelt was properly fixed and held on the seat in front to help steady herself. At one point she had to close her eyes… she had never moved at this speed and in traffic. After ten amazing minutes of advanced police driving, they filtered out onto the M23 slip road and headed south. Mike was expecting to see a big queue but it seemed to have eased, meaning that Bedford would be well on his way south now.

Clearing a hundred and twenty miles an hour in thick traffic was scary and again Michelle found herself closing her eyes. She glanced at Royston who looked very pale. She nudged him. "Are you sure you're OK?"

He blinked as if trying to wake himself up. "Yeah. Yeah. I'm Ok. Just tired. Where are we?"

Michelle realised that Mike was not OK and seemed to be fading fast. Taking a bottle of water from her bag she offered some to him.

He took a swig which seemed to revive him a little. He drank the whole bottle. "I think I'm dehydrated , Michelle."

She put an arm around him. "Well hang on in there love. It'll all work out."

Mike suddenly slowed. He spoke to his team. "The bogey's up front guys. The black Mercedes GLB… plates… SOU 688. I want you to discreetly encircle his car and bring it to a halt on the hard shoulder with two cars ready to jump him if he tries to escape."

The team acknowledged their plans and the race slowed to a crawl as they hit another traffic queue. Mike again gave instructions. "Don't move in yet. Wait until we've got room to manoeuvre. We'll probably try it when the M23 goes into the A23.

Slowly the traffic eased as drivers realised they were all bunching. "OK. Team let's go… no lights or sirens and don't look over a them at all. No clues that we are after them please."

It all seemed amazingly routine as they gradually encircled the Mercedes. They were just about to snap the trap shut by slowing in front of the SUV, when it suddenly sped off. The team followed and then the Mercedes suddenly braked violently in front of a line of cars which all braked abruptly and crashed into one another. Unfortunately the whole road was blocked and Mike's team were stranded, watching the Mercedes speed off into the distance..

Mike sat back and closed his eyes. "Shit…shit…shit. How the hell did they know we were following. Great driving on their part… but now we are stuffed." He contacted base to apprise them of what had happened and asked the helicopter teams to follow the Mercedes and see where they went. Inching the car past the crashes, blue light flashing, eventually they were clear. "All except number two car, please return to base. We'll take it from here. Can you let me know where they are please?"

The answer came back a few minutes later. "They have turned onto the A27 heading East possibly toward Newhaven or Eastbourne. The former probably… there's a ferry due out soon.. about an hour and a half's time."

"OK." Mike closed the channel. "That's possible, because we may not be able to get there and find them before it leaves… then we'll be heading for France and they do not like British police activity on their patch."

The tension was again rising. Michelle forced herself to breathe slowly and calm down. "I'm not looking forward to this, Royston… at all."

He squeezed her arm. "Me neither, but we must rescue Lucy."

CHAPTER TWENTY SIX.

Mike's speaker phone crackled. "They're going down the country road to Newhaven. Through Rodmell and Piddinghoe."

"OK. It's getting dark now, so can you keep us updated as often as possible, please." Mike re-focused on the road ahead. "Let's catch them before they can leave the country."

He accelerated and flicked on the blues. Turning off the A23 onto the A27, Mike nearly missed his exit, having to go twice round the roundabout before hitting the right road. As they turned off towards Newhaven, a message came through. "The car has been driven onto the ferry. Due to leave in twenty minutes… you should be able to get there. We'll try to delay them but generally that's not possible because of docking costs."

"What even in a case of National Security ? " Mike was surprised.

"The Harbour is French owned and the ferry company is French so no national interest there." The link closed.

The road ahead was all twists and turns. Mike had to focus intensely and knock his speed back so as not to crash. Luckily the road was mostly clear apart from the occasional slow car which quickly tucked in to let them pass. Finally, coming into Newhaven, they raced around the ring road and headed for the harbour. There was the ferry, still in port but clearly ready to depart with the loading door closed and the engines throbbing. Mike drove straight up to the customs gate and flashed his warrant card. We need to find someone on the ferry before it goes.

"Yes, that's fine. We've been informed. Go straight ahead Mr McCarthy. They have left the pedestrian boarding plank in place for you."

"Thanks." He turned to Michelle and Royston. "You two stay in the car. I don't want you in danger's way if anything happens." Mike drove along the quay and parked as close as he could to the gang-plank. He jumped out and ran up onto the ferry.

The ship security staff were waiting. "We've found the car, but not the occupants. We've looked everywhere and we don't think they are on board."

Mike frowned. "They must be… if the car's here."

"Well, we've run a full search and they aren't here. I suppose they could have gone down into the engine area but no-one has seen anyone down there, and anyway they would have needed security codes to go through the doors."

The ferry's First Officer butted in. "I'm sorry folks but we must go or we'll miss the tides and our docking place in France."

Mike thought on his feet. "I'll try to get the coast guard to give us a lift to France either in an RIB or helicopter... you can get going if they agree to do that. Our fugitives can't get off mid-channel so we've about four hours to get to Dieppe."

The First Officer nodded. "OK I'll ask the Coast Guard to contact you, asap. What's your car's radio call sign?"

"Oh, just get them to communicate through Scotland Yard… I'm DCS Mike McCarthy of the Met."

"OK. Will do. I'll get onto that immediately." He left.

Mike disembarked and returned to the car where Royston and Michelle were eager for news.

"Have you collared them, Mike?"

"No. They don't seem to be on board. No sign of them." Mike shook his head. "Bedford really is a cunning bastard. Always seems to be one step ahead of us." The car went silent. "We've got to wait for the coast guard to get us over to France."

The radio blipped. "Hello. McCarthy here."

"This is the Coast Guard at Newhaven. We have been told that you need a rapid trip across to France. We could use the 'copter but the French will take a dim view of that and it'll take ages to get the paperwork done. . It's best we go across by RIB, if that's OK. We actually have one ready in Newhaven. That's where you are, isn't it."

"Yes we're at the ferry terminal. That'd be great." Mike felt a pang of optimism. "Where do we need to meet you?"

"Opposite to you is the RNLI lifeboat station. I'll guide the team there, so get yourself to the opposite bank of the river and they'll be waiting. Probably be there in ten minutes."

"Thanks." Mike gunned the car into action and left the harbour at speed, arriving at the RNLI station further along the harbour on the West bank.

They were met by the permanent officer in charge of the station. She asked them to park away from the access road and then directed them down the lifeboat ramp to a large inflatable, sitting there with a team of four sailors on board and the engine gurgling. "Hop in and put your waterproofs and lifejackets on. There are tethers in the centre... " The captain pointed at the anchor points. "This will be a bumpy ride." The crew helped them put their protection on and then un-looped the hawser and threw it into the back of the boat.

The three of them did as they were told and secured themselves in the centre of the vessel. Initially it cruised steadily out towards the channel. "This is going to be a doddle," Royston thought. How wrong he was. As the RIB left the harbour there was a steady West to East wind blowing across in front of them. The waves suddenly seemed like mountains and the boat slammed down regularly into the troughs and then back up into the peaks. Royston and Michelle gripped the central rails for dear life. It felt as if they would be catapulted into the sea at any moment.

The vessel's captain turned back towards them. "Hold on tight. It feels worse than it is. It'll be a wee bit bumpy for a while."

Michelle grimaced. "I think that's stating the bleeding obvious." The hull slammed down on another wave. "My backside is going to be mashed after this."

The captain called back again. "It's going to get a bit rougher in a moment. We're crossing the wake of a large tanker in about three minutes."

If Michelle and Royston had thought the sea was rough, up until then, they were sorely mistaken. As the RIB hit the first of the wake waves it lifted high and plummeted steeply down about ten feet into the trough. "Holy shit. This is terrifying." Michelle was starting to feel battered.

"Hang on love," Royston shouted as they hit another huge wave. Two or three minutes later the comparative calm of the channel was restored. He shook his head. "I wish they'd given us a helicopter."

The only saving grace of this tortuous journey was that the sheer darkness of the channel gave them a spectacular view of the sky. The star speckled firmament could be seen with clarity, a view simply not visible from the light polluted shore. For a moment the sea fell flat and the sight of the Milky Way stretching overhead, was truly beautiful.

Bang. Another set of bow waves, luckily this time smaller. "This must be the shipping lane going East. That means we'll hit the lane going West after this." The waves subsided giving the occupants of the RIB a welcome break from being bashed around in all directions. Royston was looking ahead, expecting to be able to see the French coast. Instead he could see a small flashing light bobbing around some way ahead of them. "Must be a fishing vessel," he thought, dismissing its importance. He pointed it out to Michelle.

"There'll be no fishing boats out here… its in the West lane for shipping by the looks of it." She paused. "You don't think it's Bedford trying to slip across to France by the back door?"

Royston had to admit that as the unknown vessel seemed to be on the same route as their RIB, it was actually possible it was the fugitive. A long shot though, he thought. He called out to Mike. "Can you see that small boat in the distance with the intermittent light flashing." He pointed to where the light could be seen.

Mike shielded his eyes and peered into the gloom ahead. "Yes. I can see it now."

"Michelle thinks it could be Bedford heading for the coast. A long shot I know, but looking at his course compared to ours, he'll land north of Dieppe by some distance." Mike shouted forward to the Captain, asking him to track the smaller boat and catch it up if possible. The boat lurched forward with a burst of acceleration, bouncing harder on the waves as it raced forward. Slowly the small light drew nearer and the shadow of another but smaller RIB could be seen intermittently against glinting starlight reflected in the waves. Mike borrowed some binoculars and tried to focus them on the vessel ahead. They were bouncing about so hard, Mike couldn't get a view for long enough to see who was on board.

The Captain, turned off his lights so as not to warn the other boat of their arrival. At speed he directed his boat in an arc to overtake at distance and then pull in front to cut it off. The manoeuvre made Michelle suddenly feel sick, and it was all she could to retain the contents of her stomach. She closed her eyes and tried to relax and go with the rolling motion.

Suddenly she was aware of search lights blazing forward towards a small RIB heading straight towards them. The Captain spoke over his loud hailer. "This is the Coast Guard. Please stop and identify yourself."

For the first time, Royston could make out a man who was at the helm and a woman sat still in the rear centre of the boat. Immediately he recognised Jonathan Bedford. Despite him being clothed in waterproofs and a life jacket, he was easily identifiable. Simultaneously, Bedford must have seen Mike and Royston. He swerved violently to the side and sped off at right angles to the Coast Guard's vessel, which responded instantaneously, turning and following the smaller boat. The search lights blazed ahead and caught Bedford's boat zig-zagging across the line and making several rapid turns trying to evade being captured.

The Coast Guard's boat was much faster and after about twenty minutes of ducking and diving, Bedford came to a halt. The coast guard warily approached and came along side. As they did so Bedford lunged forward, a large knife glinting in the lights. He slashed at the soft sides of the RIB as hard as he could. The bigger vessel veered away out of reach at the same time as Bedford was in mid swing. He overbalanced and fell forward out of the boat, only holding on to the safety rope around the top of his RIB, with his free hand. As he landed in the water, he was twisted around and lost his grip, being pushed under the water by a wave surge.

The team on the Coast Guard vessel were busy patching the damage made by Bedford's knife, but the craft was cellular, meaning that he would have had to have punctured a dozen cells to make any serious impact on its buoyancy.

Royston could see Bedford struggling to regain his boat, but every time he tried to board it the sea washed him back. A large wave struck and Bedford disappeared in the gloom outside the range of the spotlights.

Frantically the Coast Guard circled looking for him. Nothing. Again they circled. The Captain shook his head. "He's gone, Mike. Probably taken by an under-tow. In this weather he'll only last a few minutes... it's bloody cold in the sea even at this time of year. He's a drowning man. We'll make one more sweep, but before that we'll make sure the woman on the boat is brought onto ours."

"Royston's thoughts were jolted back to Lucy. He had assumed it was her but had been more focused on what Bedford was doing. "Mike. We need to get Lucy. It looks as if she's bound to the centre railing."

"The team here will fetch her and make sure she's OK."

The crew lashed the smaller boat to the side of their own. Royston and Michelle looked on as Lucy, who was obviously drugged and limp, was unbound and carefully transferred to the bigger boat. She was laid out and wrapped in thermal blankets to stop hypothermia setting in. She opened her eyes slightly, giving Royston a weak smile. He put his arm around her. "You're safe now, Lucy. We'll get you back to shore as quick as we can." He smoothed her hair and laid her head back down. He felt terrible that this had happened to her.

His revery was broken by Michelle coming close. "How is she?"

"OK. Obviously shocked and not really conscious... but I think she'll recover."

The boat spurted into action and circled the area slowly, sweeping the search-lights across the surface in one last attempt to find Bedford. They found nothing and after an hour recorded their actions with the French and British Coast Guard HQ's and made for Newhaven, with Bedford's RIB in tow.

Arriving back at the RNLI station they all disembarked.

"I'm absolutely knackered, Michelle."

She nodded. "Me too."

An ambulance was ready and after the paramedics had given them a quick examination, they sped off to Eastbourne General. Mike followed after he'd briefed his team in London.

All three were admitted for observation overnight. Royston was given a massive dose of antibiotics , had his wounds stitched and given a blood and saline drip. They all had private rooms. Michelle felt that she needn't stay, but was persuaded by the duty doctor that she might have delayed shock but at worst needed rest up and recover.

Mike checked that they were alright. "We'll talk tomorrow. I'll send a car to collect you and take you home. Shall we say ten in the morning?"

"Make it eleven, Mike. I expect they'll need to check the wounds." Royston was struggling to stay awake. "Thanks Mike. I think this is at an end, thank god."

The quiet and stillness of the hospital was bliss. Sleep came with no prompting.

CHAPTER TWENTY SEVEN.

Royston awoke feeling a hundred percent better. Admittedly a bit battered but feeling that a weight had been lifted off his shoulders. He wolfed down his hospital breakfast and waited for the doctor's visit.

He was poked and prodded and the students accompanying the main man asked daft questions which he politely answered. Enduring all with a smile, he truly was happy to be alive and nearly in one piece. The bullet wound was starting to ache but even that was tolerable. Obviously the damaged muscle didn't work very well, but as it was his left arm, it didn't seem to interfere too much with normal existence.

Burdened with a big bag of pharmaceuticals, he sat waiting for Mike's team to pick him and the girls up. Sitting there, he mused on all that had happened over the last few weeks, trying to put it behind him and look to the future. He realised that Michelle would now be an important part of his life, even permanent. He had a deep emotional attachment that could only lead in one direction. Sincerely hoping that his feelings were mirrored in Michelle, he determined to suggest that they lived together to see if they could live long-term compatibly. Michelle was clearly still fragile about her recent marriage breakup, but she genuinely seemed to be happy to be out of it. But, he realised, that didn't mean she wanted to get re-attached immediately.

Royston was still thinking about this, when Mike appeared with two colleagues.

"Morning, hero." He laughed. "Or should I say wounded soldier."

"Hi, Mike. How are you today. Pretty tough evening wasn't it?" He struggled to stand, suddenly feeling dizzy. He sat, relaxed for a minute and tried again, this time managing to make it fully upright. "That's an indication I need to be a bit careful, eh?"

Mike stepped forward to support him. "You've got to listen to your body, Royston. Don't rush the recovery… there's plenty of time."

Royston gathered himself and stood still, feeling his balance return. "That's better."

Mike released his arm. "There you go. My team is collecting Michelle and Lucy and are going to deliver them to Michelle's apartment. That's where we're taking you in a minute. Have you got everything?"

Royston picked up his bag. "Raring to go, Mike."

They all arrived at Canary Wharf at the same time and were deposited there in a co-ordinated action. Mike was taking no chances in releasing them from his care. "Right, you three." He stood hands on hips. "We think this whole episode is now over. But I need to fill you in with the whole story. I suggest you get comfortable and make a coffee if you want, before I start."

Michelle stood. "Everyone for coffee… Cappuccinos O.K.?" They all nodded. Several minutes later she returned and handed out the mugs. "There you go, guys." She sat in one of the arm chairs and curled her legs up.

"Well." Mike cleared his throat. "I have had first sight of a report by MI6 which has been looking at the issues from an International perspective… from the outside in. That's not part of MI5's remit. They look from the inside out. Luckily there is no hint of rogue influences in MI6's section of security as they've had several sweeps through personnel after worries of infiltration several years ago. Squeaky clean apparently." He opened his file and flicked through the papers.

Royston interjected. "I bloody well hope so after this fiasco. Reminds me of the 'reds under the beds' investigations many years ago."

Mike smiled. "We don't work like the Americans, accusing everyone of being a spy, but that means sometimes we make small mistakes."

Lucy smiled. "Some small mistake, Mike."

Mike frowned. "Yes, well… luckily it wasn't on my patch. The head of MI5 is absolutely furious and indeed he could well lose his job over this. But in actuality, between us we have busted up a huge spy ring and have been able to identify many foreign agents present and past. Many have been active or are sleepers in the West. These are being rounded up now across Europe, America and Africa. There are also some in South America, but that is no surprise as it was the focus of the Nazis after the second World War, many of whom ended up with the FSB." He sipped his coffee.

"I think we've always been a leaky secret service.... remember Burgess and McClean?" Michelle added.

"Not so much recently, and it seems the Americans, despite puffing out their chests about how secure they are, may well be very upset at this latest list which has quite a few agents in their ranks. It would seem that Sebastian Brerm Hendell and his partner Elizabet Todt were key leaders in the activities."

"That follows, or why would they have adopted such extreme measures to get rid of Turner and me." He shifted uncomfortably in the chair. "There but for the grace of God, go I. The threat of radioactive poisoning really, really scared me... I remember seeing the pictures of Litvinenko going from a lively intelligent man, to a skeleton lying in a hospital bed, in a few weeks. It was terrifying, and to have been so close to that fate..." He shuddered.

Mike nodded. "I can understand that, Royston. These people do not value life at all. They are pure ideologues and would perpetrate any hideous deed in the name of their 'ideology'. Todt has a lifetime of allegiance to that and so it would appear has Hendell. In many ways all that makes them very valuable assets for the West..."

"You've got to be joking, Mike." Royston shook his head. "They couldn't possibly bring those bastards under the West's wing… surely. They should be banged up for life for the damage they've done to many many people."

"Sorry, Royston. That is exactly what they will do. There'll be a long period of forced debriefing and negotiation. To and fro, from the security services to the captives, and it will probably end with the West offering a safe haven for Todt and Hendell, secure new names and ID's and plenty of many to enable them to live a happy life."

"That's disgusting… absolutely disgusting." Lucy was angry. "How can MI5 justify helping these murdering bastards? It's totally out of order. It makes me wonder whether we have any morals at all in Government."

"To be fair, Lucy. This is not government but international security. It all works independent of politicians except at a very trivial level. It works the other way round with government being led and informed by the security services who have fingers in all pies throughout the world."

Michelle sat forward. "So that means that having been infiltrated by Todt and her team, our MI5 must be in the dog house… as usual. But how did Jonathan Bedford become entangled?"

"That's still being investigated, Lucy." Mike, sipped his coffee to lubricate his throat. "Our initial thoughts… and I must emphasise initial, seem to imply that he was being blackmailed and for some time. It is looking as if he was compromised during a trip to Istanbul many years ago and was given the choice of playing ball with Todt's team or losing his whole lifestyle and work. It looks as if he accepted his thirty pieces of silver. The security services knew he'd been bribed and used him to feed misinformation through Todt to the FSB."

"So Bedford was actually a double agent… apparently headed up his MI5 desk but actually working for the FSB." Royston frowned. "So why did he run rather than striking another double or triple bargain?"

"That we don't know, Royston. So there is still a lot to work out and there may be even more strands to this than we currently know. Incidentally, Bedford's body washed up on a beach in France and it appears he had a pocket full of memory sticks with all sorts of secret information… so it looks as if he intended to flee to the East and carry on his murky business. A really nasty piece of work to be sure."

"Well I for one don't want to get anywhere near that world again." Lucy shuddered. "I don't mind investigating crime but this… is way beyond my pay grade. I can't imagine why our Services would even contemplate working with people such as Todt who has ruined so many lives."

Royston agreed. "A bit dramatic, Lucy, but I agree entirely. I want to keep well away from the Todts of this world.

Mike clasped his hands. "I'm afraid that world security doesn't work in a pleasant way. Every

Country has a service dedicated to take advantage of any small or large chink in the armour of their neighbours. Essentially it is a two or even three faced world where nothing is what it seems, no-one is who you think they are and your national safety depends on blackmail, coercion and villainy. The people you think are your friends are your enemies and the people you think are your enemies will be your allies. It is a world of anything goes." Mike paused. "I'll give you all another briefing next week. Hopefully by then we'll know where we are with everything that has happened. Or at least we'll be able to see the broader picture. One thing is sure, Hendell and Todt will be explicitly banned from getting anywhere near you. Part of any deal will be their guaranteed acquiescence in the protection that will now surround you on a permanent basis."

Michelle looked surprised. "Surely we're not going to have security agents tailing us all the time?"

"No, Michelle. It simply means that if anyone mentions any of you or your name pops up on the Internet, it will be flagged up and followed. You may think this is over reacting, but we just want to make sure you're safe from the spy world. You won't see us but we'll keep you safe." Mike shuffled his papers back into the folder. "I've got to go back to the office now to brief my superiors. Let me know if there is anything you need or are worried about. The docs say you all need a couple of day's rest so I suggest you do just that." He stood and picked up his jacket. "I'll be in contact."

They all sat in silence, somewhat shell-shocked by Mike's revelations and the thought that Todt and Hendell were going to be scott free and working for British Intelligence.

Royston broke the silence. "That is f'ing ridiculous. Those two have nearly killed us and MI5 expect us to just accept that all that doesn't matter."

Michelle shook her head. "That is not how I thought we all worked to keep the country safe… employing these vile people. It's beyond belief."

Lucy lightened the mood. "Well I think we should all take a short break to recuperate. How about a posh hotel in the Midlands… a bit of pampering and recuperation. Maybe one of those luxury health spas."

"No I don't fancy that. They just feed you lettuce leaves and smother you with alternative therapies, all at a ridiculous cost. I'd prefer a country hotel and a bit of fine dining." Royston looked at Michelle.

"Since neither of you agree, I'll choose and you can put up with it." Let's go out to eat tonight and I'll do a bit of research now and choose a break for us all. Not too far away and with everything we need to bring us back to life." Michelle looked at each of the others. "Yes?"

All agreed. Lucy and Royston wanted to rest up until the late afternoon and then go for food locally at a local seafood restaurant in Cabot Square, a stone's throw away.

"Great idea, guys. Whatever. I'm going to bed." Royston was dog tired and his arm was aching badly. He downed some strong pain-killers and lay on his bed. He was still thinking about the Germans when he drifted off into a troubled sleep.

He slept right through to the next morning. Not too early, Royston woke with a start.

"Wakey wakey." Michelle gently nudged his shoulders. "Time to get up, Royston. You missed dinner last night."

"Uh." He rubbed his eyes and rolled over onto his back. "Ouch." He held his shoulder and drew breath. "Can't I stay here a bit longer?"

"No. We've got to get going… back to work. Or at least you have. The business won't run itself, and if we want to go away for a break, you need to tie up any loose ends."

Royston sat up and yawned deeply. "OK. I'll shower and wake myself up." Heaving himself carefully out of bed, he staggered through to his shower. Letting the warm water run over his aching body was a sheer delight. Some minutes of bliss later he dried off, shaved and dressed, feeling altogether happier with life.

Lucy and Michelle were sitting down at the breakfast bar eating toast and honey. Royston looked on envious. He realised that he was ravenous. Sliding four slices of bread into the toaster he impatiently waited the three minutes it took to create golden brown toast which popped up on cue. Placing it on a plate he applied copious honey. It tasted glorious and disappeared in a very few bites.

"Well ladies, we have a lot to sort out." He licked his thumb where a blob of honey had dribbled. "I don't think any of us anticipated any of the last few weeks happenings, but between us we have come through it all in one piece… working as a team…" He paused. "So I have a suggestion." He looked at his audience.

Lucy looked quizzical. "What's your master plan then, Royston?"

"I think we could work together as a new team, part of a new detective company even. With all our skills pooled and working together we could really make a formidable group."

Michelle looked pensive. "Actually, I've been thinking of bailing out of my current commitments and just keeping a directorship in my present company. Computing is rapidly becoming a young person's field and rather than gradually becoming a dinosaur, I think I'd be better shifting sideways in business." She smiled. "Not only that, I think it'd be fun and a very exciting challenge to work with you two."

"Oh thanks, Michelle." Lucy laughed. "I love you too."

"Seriously, If you'd like to consider us working together, I think it would be a real crack… also a great move for all of us. I'm happy to plough in some cash as a starter, but we already have the office and some good clients." Royston was really enthusiastic thinking through the possibilities. "I suggest we take our short break and get back to sort out the way forward.

"That sounds a plan." Michelle liked the idea of refreshing her self with a mini-holiday before facing the real world again. "I'll talk to my team and see if we can work out how to make this happen… and Lucy could you feed me some basic information about your company. I know my accountant will ask all sorts of questions, so I need to be ready with the answers."

"Of course, Michelle. I'll get onto that straight away, and er… Royston, can you take a first look at what we need to do to upgrade the company?"

The rest of the day was taken up returning to the office and catching up with emails, post and decisions that were overdue. They were also working on taking the first decision about their new potential detective agency. A company name.

Lucy came with up with 'Fox, Strike and Baxter', which they agreed sounded exactly right. It was modern but still with gravitas.

Royston was starting to feel less than par. Trying to lively himself up, he sat at his desk and booted his computer, started the VPN and logged onto the news. He was interrupted by Lucy shouting through to him.

"Royston. I've got some potential business on the phone. Do you want to speak to him?"

Royston stirred his brain into action and picked up his extension.

"Hello. Is that Royston Fox?"

Royston didn't recognise the caller. "Yes this is Mr Fox."

"I hope you can help. My wife is missing…"

Before the caller could say anything else, Royston cut in. "I'm sorry, we no longer deal with missing persons." He returned the receiver and sat back in his chair. "Particularly not missing German wives. Once bitten twice shy," he smiled.

End

Printed in Great Britain
by Amazon